Gay Love & Other Christmas Magic

Dylan James

Winnipeg, Canada

Published December 2019 by Deep Hearts YA, an imprint of Deep Desires Press and Story Perfect Inc.

Deep Hearts YA
PO Box 51053 Tyndall Park
Winnipeg, Manitoba R2X 3B0
Canada

Visit deepheartsya.com for more great reads.

Gay Love & Other Christmas Magic

Chapter One

Jordan

EVEN THOUGH I DIDN'T NEED TO CALL a taxi for another hour or two, I was in full-on panic mode. I shoved all my clothing into my suitcase—far more than I really needed for a week and a half back home. It's when I tried to cram my flip-flops into the middle of the pile that I finally forced myself to slow down.

I didn't need flip-flops for Christmas break.

Why the hell didn't I start packing yesterday? Leaving it until two hours before going to the airport certainly wasn't my smartest decision. I stared at the suitcase—not only did I pack my flip-flops, I also had two pairs of shorts tucked underneath my crumpled shirts. It'll be just below freezing and there's already snow on the ground back home in Virginia; I won't be wearing shorts.

"I need to start over," I muttered. I turned my suitcase upside down and dumped it all out. My bed was covered in a pile of clothing, but it didn't really look any messier than it usually is. I don't know how my roommate puts up with me, to be honest.

"Ten days," I told myself. "I'm going home for ten days."

Besides, I was going *home*, where there was a free-to-use washer and dryer. If I somehow spilled turkey gravy over everything I owned, I could wash it all. I didn't need fifteen different shirts for ten days at home. Besides, I had left a handful of sweaters and shirts in my bedroom closet at home. I could probably go with just my underwear and socks and I would have been fine.

I abandoned my suitcase and the pile of clothing on my bed and went to the window to watch the snowfall. Until today—Christmas Eve—we hadn't had much snow here in New York City. It was my first winter in the Big Apple and I guess I expected something a little more Christmassy. I mean, until this dumping we were getting today.

For it not even being noon, the sky was almost black with thick clouds. The snowflakes were fat and heavy and so numerous I couldn't really see clearly across the quad to the dorms on the other side.

Normally, this was my favorite view. I was in this dorm and clear on the other side was my boyfriend Benjamin. We sometimes sat in our windowsills so we could see each other while we texted cute things to each other. But when I needed Benjamin the most—because he always had a way of calming me down and thinking rationally and would have talked me out of this suitcase crisis—he wasn't here.

We were both going home for Christmas break, but with his parents buying his ticket with points and my parents buying mine on a seat sale, we were on separate flights. I pulled out my phone and, as I suspected, there weren't any more messages from Benjamin. By now he'd be in the air and probably watching some movie on the plane.

I shoved the phone back in my pocket. I needed to pack.

I went back to my bed and now with my suitcase emptied again, I started with the basics—socks and underwear. From there I folded up a couple pairs of pants and half a dozen shirts. I didn't really need more than this, right?

"Something's missing," I muttered. I stood back and looked at it all—the suitcase, the mess on the bed, the general mess on my side of this dorm room. I even glanced behind me to the far tidier side where my roommate Riley kept his stuff. He finished his exams early and had left the city three days ago, giving me lots of peace and quiet to study for my last exam I had yesterday. It also gave me privacy to have Benjamin over for some private time. We spent last night cuddling while watching Netflix.

No matter where I looked, I couldn't figure out what was missing. And there was *definitely* something missing.

"Benjamin's gift!" I blurted as I realized what I was searching for.

Yanking open the top drawer of my dresser, I found the gift. I carefully lifted it out of the drawer and paused to look at it. Encased in a Plexiglas box was a miniature New

York Giants-branded football with half a dozen signatures scrawled across it. As soon as I saw this in the mall, I knew I had to have it for Benjamin. It took a couple months of saving up for it, but he was worth it.

It's moments like this I still sometimes struggled to believe how my life turned around so completely in so short a time. A year ago today, back in senior year of high school, Benjamin was barely talking to me. Then on New Year's Eve, supposedly-straight Benjamin surprised me with a kiss at the stroke of midnight. From there we had months of on and off where things were going good and then they got trashed. It became too much for me. I could respect Benjamin wanted to stay in the closet, but the way he was treating me because of that just became too difficult. I broke it off with him. And then at prom he came out to our whole graduating class and declared his love for me.

Since then, we've basically been inseparable.

In other words, he was worth the exorbitant amount of money I spent on this autographed football. I put the gift in the center of the suitcase and stared at it for a moment. I was trying to envision my suitcase getting beaten up and tossed around by the luggage handlers and what that might mean for this football. My suitcase was one of those hard-sided ones and it had gotten pretty roughed up on the journey here. If it got similar treatment on the way home, that Plexiglas box could get cracked.

My gaze moved to the excessive clothing I still had in a messy pile on my bed. I picked up random pieces of clothing and wrapped them tight around the Plexiglas box, padding it and hopefully protecting it from a not-too-gentle airport employee.

In the end, almost everything I had shoved in my suitcase before I dumped everything had made its way back into the suitcase. Except for the flip-flops and shorts. I zipped the suitcase closed.

My heart was racing and I didn't know why. Maybe it was because it was getting closer and closer to my time to go to the airport…which meant I was closer to seeing Benjamin and having him in my arms again. My heart ached at the thought of seeing him again. Damn, I have it bad for the boy. I mean, we've been apart for longer than we were right now, but maybe it was the distance between us at this very moment that was getting to me.

It was also our first Christmas together—like, as a couple—so I was giving myself forgiveness for being perhaps a little too clingy. This was all new to me and I wanted it all to go well. I wanted this to be one of those Christmases to remember, where everything was perfect—building snowmen, kissing under the mistletoe, building a gingerbread house, exchanging gifts on Christmas morning…

As I stared at my suitcase, I again wondered if I had spent too much on his gift. We didn't talk about price limits for the gifts we'd buy each other, but I doubt he'd spent as much as me. That didn't bother me at all, because it's not the value of the gift that was important, but I'm worried it might make Benjamin feel like he didn't do enough for me for Christmas. What if I ended up hurting his feelings with this great gift?

God, why did this have to be so stressful?

Since my suitcase was packed, I left my dorm room and wandered the halls. I needed to keep my feet moving, find something to occupy my mind, get distracted by a distraction. Before I really knew where I was going, I realized my feet had taken me in the direction of Mandy, my bestie from the Rainbow Club. Mandy and her girlfriend London hung out with Benjamin and I quite a bit and we'd gotten to know each other quite well.

They're in a similar situation to Benjamin and I—though their home is in a different state than ours, London and Benjamin went to the airport this morning, and Mandy and I are catching a cab together.

Her door was open a crack when I approached it and I could hear her muttering to herself. I knocked lightly.

"Jordan?" she called out.

I pushed the door open. "How'd you know it was me?"

She laughed and from the sound of it I could tell she was super stressed. She had her curly red hair tied up behind her head and her cheeks looked flush with stress as she looked over her shoulder at me. "There's like no one left on campus besides you and me."

Our dorm building was basically a ghost town as of yesterday. I think I saw two people in addition to Mandy.

As I entered her room, I saw we were alike in even more ways than I ever realized. Her bed was covered in a messy pile of clothes and her suitcase was sitting in the middle of it all. Empty. I searched her bed for a pair of flip-flops, but couldn't find any. As stressed as she might've been, she was more clear-headed than me.

I pointed at the pile of clothes and said, "I've been having the same problem. I realized I was overdoing packing when I tried to shove shorts and flip-flops in there."

She looked at me over her shoulder again, but now there was a sparkle in her eye. She might've still been stressed, but she was one of those eternally happy people. It took a lot to really get her down and not much to get her up again.

"I need to just do this, don't I?" she said with determination.

She undid her hair and then used the band to tie it tighter against the back of her head. I've seen her do that many times before—tie and retie her hair—it was usually a sign she was about to do something that needed concentration. Quite often our study hangouts didn't really start until she tied her hair up.

From there, she started methodically packing her suitcase in much the same fashion as me. Underwear, pants, shirts.

"And your gift for London?" I prompted. I hadn't seen anything gift-like go in the suitcase.

"It's at home with my parents," she said as she zipped up her suitcase. "I ordered an engraved pendant I know she'll love."

"That sounds awesome," I said. London was definitely a girl that loved her jewelry; I was sure she'd love Mandy's gift. I pulled out my phone to look at the time. "We should probably call a cab now, huh?"

"I'm ready if you are. We might be heading a bit early, but it's either we wait here or we wait there."

"I don't know about you, but I'm ready to just give up on this packing and hope I've got everything I need. Less stress that way," I said. "We've both got our gifts for our partners and that's really the most important thing."

She took one last look around her room, then nodded. "Yeah, let's go."

I picked up her suitcase for her. "Come on." We walked back to my room and then I did one last similar check to ensure I hadn't forgotten anything. Satisfied, Mandy called us a cab.

I couldn't help but still fret over stuff while she made the call. I opened my dresser drawers one at a time, searching through my stuff, making sure there was nothing important I was forgetting. It all seemed good until I get to the bottom drawer—I found the other gifts I'd bought. I didn't have much because I spent too much on Benjamin's gift, but also, I didn't have time to do a lot of shopping. The only thing that would be worse than the measly gifts I got my friends and family would be forgetting them here in New York.

I let out a swear under my breath and scooped out the gifts. My family wanted New York stuff, so there was an *I Heart NY* sweater for Bella, a set of coasters with landmarks for my mom, and a couple books on the history of the city for dad. And then there was the gift for Hannah and Kumail. I hadn't seen my BFF and her BF since we all packed up and left for school. Her and her beau went to the west coast while Benjamin and I went to the east. There was a whole country between us. For them, I got gift cards for a dinner and movie date.

I'd texted and snapped Hannah frequently and had a few video calls with them, but that wasn't anywhere close to being in the same room and talking without technology. I haven't hugged my BFF in months. We badly needed a catch-up session.

Pack—right, I needed to pack. I opened the suitcase and pulled out some of the useless clothes that were just there for padding Benjamin's gift, and in the now-open space, I tucked in the rest of these gifts. I zipped it all closed and I desperately hoped I wasn't forgetting something else.

"What the hell?" Mandy said. Her voice was loud and I could hear a note of panic in her tone.

"What is it?" I said, turning around. She still had her cell pressed to her ear. She held up her index finger, silencing me.

"Completely?" she asked. Her voice was softer now, but there was still panic there. She paced the room like a panther in a cage. "Like, *totally* completely?"

"Mandy?" I said, stepping closer. Something was wrong. Really wrong.

She just held up her index finger again, wordlessly begging me to be quiet just a little longer. She paced over to the window and glared through the glass; that couldn't be a good sign. "So, it won't help if I call someone else?"

"Someone else?" I blurted out, earning me another

index finger begging for silence. *Someone else? They can't take us to the airport?*

Mandy turned away from me and sighed and muttered a few words, then stabbed the disconnect button on her phone. She hugged herself and a tremor ran through her body.

"Mandy?" I said. I stepped closer to her and put a hand on her back. She turned and buried her face against my neck, crying softly. I hugged her. "What's wrong?"

She sniffled, then backed up a step and ran her hands over her face. Her gaze flickered from my face to somewhere behind me. *The window*, I realized.

"The blizzard has basically shut down the city. The snow is too deep for most cars and even if they could make it through the snow, there's a ton of stalled cars all over the place. There's no way to get to the airport."

I hurried over to the window. "It *can't* be that bad," I said, though I didn't know if I was trying to convince her or myself. But even as I tried to tell my eyes what I was seeing wasn't that bad, I could tell it was. Someone was walking across the quad—though I'd really hesitate to call it walking, given the almost-knee-deep snow and the awkward giant steps they had to take. The snow also collected in drifts, lower in some areas, but higher in many more.

"No," I said, still not sure who I was trying to convince. I marched past Mandy and into the hallway. I broke out into a near-run to make it to the small lounge at the end of the hall where there were windows that overlooked a nearby traffic intersection. Surely there were still cars out and about; the cab company had to have been wrong. It couldn't be that bad. There must be a way to get to the airport.

"Jordan?" Mandy called as she came running after me. Our footsteps echoed up and down the hall.

I came to a halt when I reached the windows. The street below was just as snow-laden as the quad and in the middle of the intersection were three cars that were obviously turned off and abandoned. Snow piled on top of them, covering them from view.

I pressed my face against the window, desperate to see down the street, hoping beyond hope to find some cars. Anything.

Nothing. There was nothing.

It felt like my knees gave out. I grabbed the railing in front of the window to stop myself from completely collapsing, but I eased myself down to the floor and buried my face in my knees.

"Christmas is ruined," I said.

Mandy sat beside me and put an arm over me, pulling me close in a side-hug. I expected her to tell me everything would be all right. Instead, she said, "Christmas sucks."

I couldn't help but chuckle, but it didn't make me feel any better. Instead, I felt worse the more I thought about it. I wouldn't see my family or Hannah or Kumail—not to mention Benjamin. It was supposed to be our first Christmas together. It was supposed to be romantic. We were supposed to do the cute things couples do at Christmastime—like kiss under the mistletoe, decorate Christmas cookies, watch Hallmark movies while drinking eggnog. We had all these plans to make it *perfect*, and now all those plans were ruined.

You only had your first Christmas once. You could only make those memories once. There were no do-overs.

And my first Christmas with Benjamin was now an epic fail with no hope of recovery.

Chapter Two

Benjamin

I DRUMMED MY FINGERS AGAINST ONE knee while the other knee bounced impatiently. *How long are we going to be stuck on the tarmac?* I looked through the window again and, if anything, it looked worse than it did an hour ago…when we were still sitting on the tarmac.

I stretched my neck and looked around the cabin. All I saw were exhausted and depressed faces.

First our flight had been delayed by an hour. Then when we eventually boarded and got seated, the captain told us we'd be delayed a little longer while airport crews cleared the runway of snow. And then we were told we'd have to wait until the weather got a little better. If we had just taken off when we were supposed to, I'd be getting home about now and preparing for Jordan to join me.

I missed my family. My parents called me weekly and sometimes they put my brothers on, but still that wasn't the same as actually being there in person with them. I missed our family dinners and missed my brothers roughhousing.

But more than anything, I was looking forward to spending Christmas with Jordan. Although, admittedly, I was a little nervous about spending the holiday with both our families again with us being the couple at the center of it all, the couple that brought these two families together. It was a lot of pressure.

Our first major holiday with our families was Thanksgiving. We'd both flown back home to Virginia for that and teamed up to cook a giant dinner for both of our combined families. Between our parents, siblings, grandparents, aunts, and uncles, there were just over thirty people at dinner. It was supposed to be a big thing—our big debut as a couple. I wanted it to be a chance to show everyone what a caring and attentive boyfriend I was.

But then my Aunt Janine showed up. She was dressed as she normally was, in a pair of slacks and a nice sweater, but dangling on top of her sweater was a giant cross necklace. I tend to think of Aunt Janine as the "Super Christian". You know, the judgy kind who quotes Bible verses now and then. Normally, that's not much of a problem, but with this being a chance to showcase my *gay* relationship and my *gay* boyfriend...well, I got a few looks from her.

Shortly after she arrived, she asked me if I'd ever read a certain passage in Corinthians. I told her no and when I faked a need to go to the bathroom so I could get a few minutes of privacy, I Googled the verse. It was clearly an anti-gay passage and my aunt was trying to tell me I was going to Hell for this. That didn't faze me—spiritually, I mean. I'm not the strongest believer, but over the summer I did read up a bit on the Bible and homosexuality and learned most of those anti-gay passages are used by certain people to twist what the Bible says. Lots of people are Christian and are fine with gay relationships.

My aunt was one of those Christians that was against gay relationships.

And that sort of shut me down for the rest of Thanksgiving weekend. I was so horribly depressed and through the whole dinner I felt like I was being judged non-stop—not just by my aunt, but by everyone. I started acting more like Jordan's friend rather than his boyfriend and I worried he was judging me as inadequate as a boyfriend.

I mean, I knew that was ridiculous. We had a chat after dinner was over and I told him everything and he said he didn't even notice how I had withdrawn all night. But I knew he was just being nice. He didn't want to hurt my feelings and tell me how he was really disappointed with me.

I stopped myself from going down this well of self-doubt and self-criticism again. Jordan and I had talked about it a few times since then and every time he did his best to convince me all he wanted from me was just me. Not a show of any sort in front of other people. Just me. Nothing else.

I exhaled and did my best to push out all of those negative feelings with my breath.

I loved Jordan with all my heart, but in addition to the

Thanksgiving fiasco, the toughness of this term of school meant I haven't been the most attentive boyfriend. I felt like sometimes I didn't measure up and I wasn't really ready to have our relationship examined by our parents and siblings. Or by my Aunt Janine.

But I knew I'd get through it all with Jordan's help. And I'd make up for being an inattentive boyfriend during the next school term. He kept telling me he knew I loved him and that school had to come first; sometimes I worry he's too good for me, that I don't deserve him.

Christmas was the chance to make it all better, to make up for everything and get us back on the right track. I know he wanted Christmas to be special since it was our first one together. For his gift, I bought us tickets to a Broadway show; we've been in New York for four months now and we haven't done any of the New York things. I wanted to treat him special and make a memorable night of it—plus, for someone who's been a rather inattentive boyfriend, a big splashy date would more than make up for all that. Right?

Anyway, at this rate, still stuck on the tarmac, Christmas was looking to be a disaster.

The only thing to make this worse would be—

The speaker system crackled and then the captain's voice spilled forth. "I'm sorry to be the bearer of bad news, passengers, but air traffic control has cancelled all flights until further notice, including ours."

A collective groan rolled through the passenger cabin, temporarily drowning out the captain. I groaned too. I mean, I had kind of been expecting this, but until he said that, I could still hold onto hope we'd take off.

"We'll be taxiing back to the terminal now. I realize this ruins Christmas for a lot of you and we deeply apologize for this. If there was any chance we could have taken off in this storm, we would have done so already."

I stopped listening to the rest of it. He went on to say something about how to get a refund on the ticket, but I just didn't care anymore. I crossed my arms over my chest and just stared at the back of the seat in front of me.

Christmas was ruined. Totally. Completely. Irreparably.

Well, I realized, *there's still one upside. Jordan.* If my plane was cancelled, then his would be too since he was supposed to take off a couple hours from now. I would still get my Christmas with Jordan. It wouldn't be the picture-perfect Christmas he wanted and we wouldn't have our families or his friends, Hannah and Kumail, or my old football buddies, but we would have each other.

That can still be a romantic Christmas, right? I mean, other than the fact we would be stuck in our sterile dorm building that was probably super empty and our Christmas dinner would likely consist of whatever we could find in the vending machines. *Nothing says Christmas like splitting a KitKat bar.* I sighed. *Think positive; I can still make up for everything and make this a good Christmas for us.*

The plane rattled and rocked as the pilot steered it back toward the terminal. When the walkway was hooked up to the plane and the door opened, they turned on all the lights to full brightness and people collectively groaned again and stood up, grabbing their bags and jamming themselves into the aisle. I grabbed my backpack and joined the masses. Like a school of fish, we moved as one off the plane and through the terminal and over to the baggage claim area.

As I waited with the disgruntled crowd for the luggage carousel to rumble to life and our bags to appear, I realized just how close we'd come to Christmas being an absolute disaster. I could deal with having a Christmas away from my family, but this early into my relationship with Jordan, I don't think I'd make it through a Christmas without him. I'd be a depressing disaster.

Jordan, I realized. *I need to text him.*

If I could reach him before he gets into a taxi, I could save him time and money—and head off him feeling like the perfect Christmas he'd been planning had been ruined. With the right words from me, Jordan would see the bright side in this—Christmas with just the two of us without the pressures and expectations of family. We could cuddle and watch Netflix again.

It'll be nice. Just me and him. And, actually, having this holiday without that subtle scrutiny of our parents and siblings—or the obvious scrutiny of my Aunt Janine—could be a good thing. We could just enjoy each other and the special day without the pressure of being the perfect couple. Jordan kept telling me not to worry about those things, but I just couldn't shake the worry that sometimes I didn't measure up.

I couldn't help but smile as I reached for my phone to text him. My pocket was empty. I patted each pocket of my jeans and then checked them all again. The pockets in my jacket were similarly empty. I yanked my backpack off my shoulder and frantically searched through every pocket and compartment. *What the hell?* I double-checked by searching all my pockets again.

A cold sweat peppered my brow. I mean, this wasn't a complete and total disaster because I didn't need my phone to make my way back to the dorm, but now I didn't have a way to contact Jordan. He'd think I was home and he was stuck here. My heart ached at the pain I knew he'd feel when he realized that.

I searched the floor around me—maybe I dropped it and didn't notice? Even as I searched, I knew that wouldn't turn up anything. A phone doesn't just magically hop out of my jeans pocket and land on the floor without me, or anyone around me, noticing.

A deep sense of panic hit me as I started walking back in the direction I came from, desperately searching for my phone, despite knowing I wouldn't find it. When I reached the security doors we came through after leaving the terminal, I finally accepted all hope was lost. The doors were opaque with shaded glass and there were big "DO NOT ENTER" signs.

I turned around to look at the crowd gathered around the still-not-moving luggage carousel. Most likely, one of them stole my phone. *Or,* I considered, *I left it on the plane.* My dad did that once—it took him over a week to get his phone back. *I'll file my report with the airline later, no point in getting worked up and wasting time now.*

Besides, what I wanted most right now was to just go home to Jordan and as fast as possible.

With all the cancelled flights, the customer service desks would be overworked and have super long lines of angry passengers. I'd be best to just go back to my dorm and file the report online.

When the luggage carousel *finally* rumbled to life, I was still down in the dumps and depressed, but I had a plan. More than that, the end of my plan—my goal—was to be in Jordan's arms again. Despite all that, I was moody and irritable and impatient.

As suitcases started appearing and rolling past on the carousel, the crowd started thinning out as they grabbed their luggage and stormed off. The mood here was horrible, like it was everything I was feeling, magnified a million times. I could certainly understand why; so many people would have been on their way home to spend Christmas with their loved ones. While I was certainly missing out on Christmas with family too, my most-loved one was still here in New York City.

Eventually my suitcase showed up. I pushed through the crowd to grab it and then headed toward the exit. As I emerged through a set of secure doors, I was assaulted by the noise of hundreds of voices, most of them shouting. I looked to the left and saw all of the angry passengers demanding this be resolved now. *Yeah, no way I'm getting my phone back today.*

I turned back to my destination—the final set of doors and the chaos of New York City beyond. But I stopped in my tracks.

Seeing the snow from the plane in the middle of the field of runways was one thing, but to see it now here in front of me as it covered cars and people and trees and stuff...wow, this storm was insanely intense.

Nevertheless, I needed to get to Jordan.

I took a moment to zip up my jacket the rest of the way and pulled my toque down over my ears and shoved my hands into a pair of gloves. As I did all of this, the snow outside went sideways for a bit—it was hella windy out there.

I grabbed my suitcase and exited the airport. The icy cold wind slammed into my face and snowflakes pelted my cheeks. I could barely open my eyes because every time I did, I got snowflakes in them. However, I could vaguely make out the taxi stand in front of me. I walked forward, making stumbling footsteps with all of the slushy snow.

After managing to reach the taxi, I opened the back door and got in. It took a moment to stop shivering and then I dusted the snow off my jacket.

The driver looked back at me. He had to be no more than a few years older than me, but with a full beard across his jaw. "Dispatch says I'm not supposed to take any fares."

"Seriously?" I asked, disbelieving. "I need to get home to my boyfriend."

After realizing I'd uttered the word "boyfriend", something I tried not to do when I didn't know if the person I was talking to was homophobic or an ally, my gaze darted toward him and then away. *Crap. I should just get out.*

As I reached for the door handle, the driver said, “Hang on. Where’s home?”

My heart hammered in my chest. I looked at him and I didn’t see the look of disgust I feared I’d see. “But what about dispatch?”

He shook his head. “Man, if I didn’t make a solid effort to get home to my man on Christmas Eve, he’d probably leave me.” He chuckled and I suddenly felt very comfortable in his presence. He was more than an ally, he was gay like me. “Now, where’s home?”

“NYU.”

His gaze drifted up to the ceiling between us and his lips moved as he muttered some words. I recognized them as street names—he was running through the route. Then his gaze snapped toward me again. “If we take all the major streets between here and there, we should be fine. The plows are out in full force.”

“Okay,” I said, suddenly smiling. This was going to work after all! Soon I’d be hugging Jordan.

The driver shifted in his seat, facing forward. “Now,” he said as he shifted into drive and pulled out of the taxi stand, “tell me about this boyfriend we’re braving the blizzard for.”

Chapter Three

Jordan

MANDY AND I SAT IN HER WINDOWsill, watching out over the snow-covered quad. The sky was still dark as night and the snow was coming down so hard it looked like TV static. I could *barely* see the dorms on the other side of the quad.

After the cab company telling us we couldn't get picked up, we did some digging on if we could get there via the subway. There was a route, but apparently everything was super delayed—and combine that with having to lug a suitcase through knee-high snow—we quickly realized that wasn't going to work. We even checked the airport website and it looked like every flight was delayed. It didn't take a genius to figure out they'd all soon be cancelled. There was no point in even *trying* to get to the airport.

The ledge under the window was just wide enough for me to sit on it and stay balanced. I had my knees pulled up against my chest, hugging them. Mandy seemed a little more relaxed in her posture—her legs were crossed at the ankles and off to the side—but it was clear from the wrinkle in her brow she was as upset as me.

"Christmas is gonna suck," I say. I'd been saying stuff like that over and over since she ended the call with the cab company. I was honestly surprised she hadn't told me to shut up yet. I leaned the side of my head against the glass; the cold seeped through and chilled my skin.

"Gonna suck so hard," she said.

I narrowed my eyes and shifted my gaze to her. That was basically the first acknowledgement from her of how sucky Christmas would be since the phone call. Like, did it take that long for it to really sink in with her?

"What?" she said when she saw me staring.

"Nothing." I sighed and got up, tugging the bottom of my shirt to straighten it out. "I should go back to my room and call my parents, let them know the bad news."

"Me too," she said, turning her head to look at her laptop lying on top of her suitcase.

I opened my arms to give her a hug and she got up off the windowsill to slide her arms around me. "Christmas is still gonna suck," I said, "but at least I've got a friend."

She made an unconvinced *mmm* sound that I tried not to take personally. I mean, I understood. The only way to salvage this was to have Benjamin here.

A moment later I was back in the hallway, making my way back to my dorm. It seemed with every step I took, it just sunk in more and more how alone I'd be this Christmas. Yeah, I'd have Mandy, but I wouldn't have mom or dad or Bella. Or Benjamin. That one hurt the most. I've had so many Christmases with my family that missing one now wasn't the end of the world, but this was the *first* Christmas with Benjamin and I as a couple and it just made my heart ache to know we'd be spending it in different states.

We'd made sure to celebrate all of the firsts that go along with being a couple—first Halloween (we dressed up as ketchup and mustard bottles), first six months together (we went to a fancy restaurant), and first Thanksgiving together (we went home and cooked a *giant* dinner for both our families). Our first Christmas together was supposed to be filled with mistletoe, gifts, time with our families, Christmas baking, and going for late night hikes in the snow-dusted park where we had one of our first dates.

Benjamin had felt our Thanksgiving had gone badly due to something his aunt had said to him, but I'd had a good time. It was really nice to just be there as a couple surrounded by our families. I knew Benjamin wanted to make Christmas extra special to make up for Thanksgiving, even though I kept telling him he had nothing to make up for.

However, thanks to this damn weather, Benjamin would spend Christmas at home with his family and I'd spend mine at school with a friend. We'd be apart. Sure, we'd video call each other on Christmas Day, but you couldn't cuddle over video, couldn't kiss, couldn't just enjoy the warmth of each other's bodies as we laid on the couch and watched a movie. I couldn't convince him all I needed for Christmas was him; I didn't need him to convince his aunt we were valid as a couple.

By the time I reached my dorm, I was fully in the depths of depression. It felt like every step I was trying to force my legs through mud and I just stared at the floor as I went along. I let myself into my dorm and sat down on my bed. I checked my phone for a text from Benjamin—surely he'd be landing soon and I know he'd text me immediately. But I had no notifications.

I pulled my laptop out of my bag and booted it up, then opened Skype. I called home.

It rang a few times and then mom answered. The video screen opened to show her with a fully-Christmased house behind her—and I instantly felt more homesick than I've felt my entire time away. Right then, the video froze on that picture of her smiling face and the beautifully lit tree behind her.

Her voice came through, though. "Hi, Jordan!" Then a moment later she was a little less cheery. "What's wrong?"

The video of her sparked to life, but then went awash in static before freezing again on a new shot of her, but with the colors all wrong. Her face was a sickly green and the Christmas tree behind her was mostly black and white.

"Have you seen the news?"

"The news? Oh, the storm? It's not that bad, right?" I could hear worry in her voice through all of the crackly static. Like she was trying to convince me everything was going to be all right even if she didn't believe it herself.

"It's bad, mom. Everything's shut down. I can't get to

the airport." There was another surge of audio static. I waited for it to dissipate. "Besides, the airport is going to be shut down any minute, I'm sure." There was a very long silence. "Mom? Did you hear that?"

After yet another wash of audio static, and with her face still frozen in that sickly green, she said, "You're breaking up, honey, but I got enough of it. Stay safe. Maybe you can fly out tomorrow or the day after. We can—" More static interrupted whatever she was about to say.

"Mom? You were cut off. We can what?" I said, speaking loudly.

"I—" Static. "—get home."

"Mom?" I practically shouted. I didn't know if raising my voice helped, but it seemed the right thing to do. "Mom! You're cutting out!"

"—stmas, Jordan—"

And then Skype cancelled the call.

I swore out loud and wanted to punch the computer. I double-clicked mom's name to start another call, but it beeped at me and said *connection failed.* I tried again with the same result. After a third *connection failed* message, I noticed the wifi icon in the corner of my screen was doing something. Though I had a strong signal, it didn't seem to be working. Just as I was about to shout something full of swears at the computer, a pop-up window said "No internet connection."

"What?" I muttered to myself. I pulled out my phone—no wifi there either, and no bars. I wasn't even getting a cell signal. I tried texting my mom anyway, but it immediately came back as undeliverable.

I shut my computer and refrained from launching it against the wall. Instead, I just put it beside me, and then put my phone next to it. I walked across the room and collapsed face-down on my roommate's bed—since it was free from clutter—and buried my face in the crook of my elbow.

I had to really work hard not to cry.

Apparently, there was one thing worse than being stuck here at school while everyone I knew was back home—unless this got fixed overnight—now I couldn't even call, text, or Skype them on Christmas Day. I was completely cut off from everyone I loved. Instead, I'd spend Christmas in this dorm with Mandy and the dozen or so international and graduate students who didn't go home for the break.

I sniffled, but still managed to not cry. But if I stayed here by myself wallowing in my self-pity, I was going to actually cry. I stood and sniffled again, wiping my sleeve across my nose, and left my dorm room. I had to find Mandy—she was the only person here that I knew and the only person that would put up with me moping about Benjamin and the only person that had a hope in hell of saving my miserable Christmas. She was also the only one who could give me a hug right now and I really needed one.

I practically ran down the hallway back toward her room. Before I even got halfway there, she came running toward me.

"The wifi's down," she shouted as we neared. She looked as grief-stricken as me.

"I know." We finally crashed into a hug. The hug felt good—it wasn't Benjamin, but it was a friend. It was human closeness. It was me not being a hundred percent alone on Christmas.

"Christmas sucks," she whimpered into my shoulder.

We hugged each other for a long time and eventually we pulled ourselves apart. I looked at my friend. We'd known each other for less than four months—we met when I first went to the Rainbow Club with Benjamin in tow and Mandy and London were there and looking for new friends. If Mandy hadn't crossed the room and shook my hand, we probably never would have really hit it off.

Sure, Mandy wasn't Benjamin, wasn't my family, wasn't Hannah and Kumail...but Mandy was still important to me. *We should make the most of this,* I told myself. We could still make Christmas at least a little bit special.

Or, at the very minimum, we should try not to have a miserable Christmas.

"Come on," I said. I spun her around and put my arm over her shoulders. I sniffled one last time and then told myself I wasn't going to cry anymore. "Hot chocolate from the vending machine is on me."

She wiped her fingers across both eyes and then looked up at me. Her eyelids were red-rimmed. "I know what you're doing."

"What am I doing?"

"You're trying to make Christmas less awful." She

took a deep cleansing breath and straightened her spine. “Thank you. And if the vending machine hot chocolate has a whip cream option, you’re getting it for me.”

Chapter Four

Benjamin

"YOU DIDN'T," THE CAB DRIVER SAID, watching me from the rear-view mirror.

I laughed. "I did. I took the mic and declared my love for him." The driver—Charlie—had asked for the story of how Jordan and I got together. Telling him the whole thing, from surprise New Year's Eve kiss to my final declaration of love and personal coming out at senior prom—had helped pass the time in the super-slow traffic.

If there were plows out clearing the streets of New York City, they were nowhere near here. The streets were a snowy, slushy mess and it was coming down so hard I don't know how Charlie managed to keep us going safely in the right direction. I could barely see anything from where I was sitting—the headlights seemed to just highlight the fat snowflakes and not shine any further than that. However, he did seem to manage and kept us going, even if at a crawl. I guess it was really just a matter of following the car in front of us; the red glow of their tail lights did make it through the falling snow to us.

"And it's been good as gold since then?" Charlie asked.

"Pretty much," I said, nodding. "I mean, we have our fights now and then like any couple does—" and here Charlie nodded and went *mmhmm* like I was speaking his experience "—but all that drama taught us we need to always communicate. Talking with each other is how we get through everything. We share everything."

I felt a pang in my heart as I said that because the one thing missing today was communication. Jordan likely had no idea I was still in the city, let alone I was on my way to him. He had to be stressed out beyond belief right now and I wasn't there to calm him down and comfort him. It gave me flashbacks to the really rocky part of our relationship when we had all those troubles. We weren't communicating—*I* wasn't communicating—and that had messed everything up. And here I was not communicating again. Though, admittedly, it wasn't my fault this time.

"Man," Charlie said, "you guys are in for a happy future together."

I smiled and tried to banish the thoughts of how losing my cell phone had mired me in a potential Christmas disaster with Jordan. I leaned back in the seat, looking out the side window, trying to distract myself. It was the afternoon and the sky was almost black with clouds and all I could see was snow. I barely had any idea where we were; it looked like we were at the North Pole at midnight.

"Well," I said, the full despair of the situation sinking in again, "if I miss our first Christmas together, I hope that's not an omen for the future."

"*What?*" Charlie said, disbelief thick in his voice. "After all that, you think missing Christmas because of the blizzard of the millennium is going to put you in the dog house? My man, you've got to trust yourself and Jordan and your relationship a lot more. Besides, *we are going to make it* to NYU and you're going to spend Christmas with your honey!"

I couldn't help but smile—Charlie's enthusiasm was infectious. "Thank you," I said. When a lull in our conversation settled over us, I asked, "What about you? You got a boyfriend at home?"

"No," he said, and for a moment I worried I'd misinterpreted what he'd said earlier. But then he added, "I have a *husband* at home, thank you very much." He winked at me in the rearview mirror.

"Sweet," I said. "Tell me about him."

"I knew Simon in high school but we got together during a volleyball tournament," Charlie said, launching into the story of his love, a giant smile on his face the whole time...

I remember when we first got to our shared hotel room and closed the door. I was terrified. I was starting to accept I was bisexual—and I had a crush on Simon. But I was certain he was as homophobic as half the guys on the team. I wasn't looking forward to spending two nights with him alone.

Simon and I didn't really get along with the other guys on the team—there was some sort of clique we weren't part of—so we just sort of decided to hole up in our room and watch some TV. That first evening was hella awkward. He turned on some sci-fi show I'd never heard of before and I had to hold back from asking him questions about everything on the show because I didn't want to annoy him. Plus, the sound of his voice makes my brain turn to Jell-O. I was so attracted to him that I was non-functional sometimes.

After the hour-long show was over, I was about to feign some sort of illness and just sit on the toilet for the next hour so I could be in a different room. But then he flipped the channels and we stumbled on an old episode of Queer as Folk. *And there were two guys kissing on the screen.*

My blood ran cold. Was Simon going to make some sort of homophobic comment? Like call them fags or something? But then he put the remote down beside him, folded his hands in his lap, and watched the scene.

"Charlie?" he asked, still looking at the TV and not at me. His voice quivered a little bit.

"Yeah?" I said.

"Do you…are you…what do you think of this scene?"

My heart was thudding against my ribs so hard I thought they might crack. Was this a set-up to an outing and a beating? Or was he trying to tell me something?

"What do you mean?" I managed to croak out.

He opened his mouth to say something, then clamped his lips shut. After a long awkward silence, he said, "Never mind."

We watched the rest of the episode and Simon seemed totally absorbed by it. When it was over, my heart was still thudding hard, only now it felt like it was lodged in my throat.

I needed to say something. Needed to tell him the truth. I didn't know why, but I knew I had to.

"Simon," I said. "I'm bi."

He looked down at his hands in his lap and examined his fingernails. I looked at those fingers too and noticed they were shaking…quivering. He was nervous.

"Me too," he whispered.

We talked the whole night about how and when we knew we were bi and all of the boys we thought were cute. Then he said, "And I think you're cute too." He was staring at his fingernails again.

My mouth fell open. Me? I couldn't quite process that. He thought I was cute?

"Um…" I said, "I kind of think you're cute too."

He looked up at me with the biggest grin ever. His smile was always one of my favorite things about him.

With that awkwardness out of the way, we cuddled and watched some more TV and totally made out late into the night. We managed to keep it a secret for the rest of the volleyball trip, but once we got back to school, one of our teammates caught us holding hands in the stairwell. He told the rest of the team and then soon the rest of the school found out. It was tough finishing off high school, but we did it. I wouldn't have survived that homophobia without Simon's support—it was brutal sometimes. I always felt like he was the solid, strong one and I was the weak one that needed support, but he didn't seem to mind it as long as I was by his side.

"…It's been almost ten years now," he said, finishing off his story. "I've been far from the perfect boyfriend or perfect husband, but Simon has always loved me anyway. I think he knows this eats away at me sometimes and so he always tries to tell me I'm perfect just the way I am." Charlie blushed. The love he felt for Simon was clear in his voice and in his eyes as I watched them in the rearview mirror.

We talked for a long time about our boys and as we began to wrap up our conversation, I realized we hadn't moved in a very long time. We'd just been sitting here. The red tail lights in front of us seemed bright and angry, like they were confronting us for speaking of same-sex attraction.

"Charlie?" I asked. I tried to keep the worry out of my voice, but I knew I failed when my voice cracked on the first word. "How far along to NYU are we?"

He looked at me in the rearview mirror before answering and I knew instantly I didn't want to hear the answer. "My man," he said, "we've barely left the airport behind; we're not even halfway to Queens."

That wasn't good. NYU was on Manhattan—the island—which was still a way to go from Queens. There were probably ten miles or more between Jordan and I. In the middle of summer, that wouldn't be an issue, but in the depths of this horrible snowstorm, ten miles could have been a hundred.

"And we haven't moved for a while, right?" That feeling of dread was sinking into the pit of my stomach again, the same feeling of dread I felt when my flight was cancelled, the same feeling that intensified by a million when I realized my phone was missing. And now it was a billion times more intense.

Charlie turned and looked at me. He seemed defeated.

"I think traffic is at a standstill. A bunch of people are probably stuck and blocking everything." He turned forward again and turned the wheel back and forth and the car shifted forward a bit as he lifted his foot off the brake. We soon rolled back an inch, settling into place. He looked at me again, even more defeat on his face. "And I think we're stuck too."

I swore under my breath. Charlie turned to face forward again and looked down. "Sorry," I said. "It's not your fault, I know."

He sighed. "I just wanted to make your Christmas perfect."

I put my hand on Charlie's shoulder. "Thank you, Charlie. You got me much further than I would have otherwise gotten. More than that, you gave me hope I can actually make it home and make this a Christmas to remember."

He beamed at me, then looked out the window and back at me. "What's your plan from here?"

I shrugged. "Subway, maybe? I certainly can't walk the whole way."

"Hmm. Some of them are down, but not all of them. I don't think we're far from a subway station—you could take that back to Manhattan; I think there's a stop only a few blocks from NYU." He pulled out his phone and opened an app. "I'm checking which subway lines are down and which are still up." He waited for it to load but nothing seemed to be happening. He swiped through a few controls and tried again. "I don't seem to be getting any data on my phone." He tapped a few more things and swiped a few more controls, then opened up his app once again. "Sorry, man. I can barely get a cell signal, never mind full data. I don't think my connection is even strong enough to send a text."

"No worries," I said. I felt guilt hit me for a brief moment; if I had been more on top of things, I could have asked to text Jordan from Charlie's phone. Now that the realization had hit, he didn't have a connection. It was almost as if everything was working against me, like I wasn't meant to get home to Jordan. *I will do it,* I told myself. *No matter what it takes, I'll do it.* "I'm going to have to just try it. If worse comes to worst, I can walk home and warm up in every McDonald's and Dunkin' Donuts I pass."

Charlie tossed his phone on the passenger seat. "I don't know, man. Walking in this weather?"

I smiled. "If this was your first Christmas with Simon, what would you do?"

He didn't even need to think about it. "I'd do whatever the hell it took to get me to him."

"Exactly."

Charlie looked ahead again, seeming to scope out the stalled traffic. I pressed my face against the window to try and see past the cars in front of us. All I saw was a sea of red taillights and then the window fogged up from my breathing. No one seemed to be moving.

I sighed. This was going to be cold and difficult, especially with trying to lug my suitcase through all that deep snow. “How much do I owe you?” I asked, pulling out my wallet.

“Nothing,” Charlie said. When he turned and saw my wallet in my hands, he shook his head. “Call it a Christmas gift. I didn’t get you far—I certainly didn’t get you to your man—but I got you a little closer, and that’s the least I can do for someone in need on Christmas Eve. The fare is on me.”

“Thank you, Charlie,” I said. I grabbed the strap of my backpack and the handle of my suitcase, ready to dash out and through the snow, but before I did, I let go of my suitcase and extended my hand. “Merry Christmas, Charlie, to you and Simon.”

He smiled broadly and took my hand, shaking it. “Merry Christmas, Benjamin, and merry Christmas to Jordan too.”

I grabbed my backpack again, half slinging it over my shoulder, in preparation for braving the storm. “The nearest station,” I said, “do you know where it is from here?”

Charlie leaned toward the passenger side of the car and pointed straight ahead. “See that intersection there? Hang a right and follow it for a couple blocks. Should be right there. Hard to miss.”

“Thank you, again. Merry Christmas.” I opened the door and stepped out into the storm. Cold wind whipped across my face and up my sleeves and up the bottom of my coat, instantly chilling me.

I hiked my backpack higher up on my shoulder and picked up my small suitcase—there was no point in trying to wheel it through all this snow—and paused to take in my surroundings before slogging through the snow. I was literally in the middle of the street with all of the cars just sitting idle like I was in some giant parking lot.

I looked to the intersection Charlie had pointed at. It was hard to see, mostly because snow kept hitting me in the eyes, forcing me to squint. When the traffic light changed to green, it became a lot easier to see through the thick flurry of snowflakes. It was like a beacon pulling me through the storm and home to Jordan.

With my free hand, I grabbed the collar of my jacket in my fist and bunched it up under my chin. It really didn't do much to counter the chilling wind, though, as it seemed to find any and every crevice in my clothing and then rushed into it.

I plodded through the snow. My shoes weren't the greatest for this kind of weather—they weren't warm, weren't waterproof, and they didn't come up higher than my ankle. After the first few steps, I already had snow in my shoes and my feet were cold and getting wet, which would only make them colder.

Get to the subway, I reminded myself. Once I got to the subway station, I'd be indoors and in the heat. I'd be in the cold again once I was in Manhattan, but that was only so I could walk the few blocks down to NYU, then I'd not only be inside and warm again, but I'd be able to put on a pair of clean, dry socks.

Warmth is not far away, I thought. I had to keep

repeating mental mantras like this one, because I was already growing miserable. The tips of my ears were really cold and starting to hurt. And after all this walking, I had barely crossed half the distance between the cab and the corner, never mind the next two blocks down to the station. I glanced behind me—I was still close enough to Charlie's cab that I could make him out when he waved at me, his silhouette outlined by the headlights of the car behind him.

Hot chocolate and, more importantly, Jordan are at the end of all this. Each step felt like an effort with all of the snow and slush.

After what seemed like forever, I finally reached the intersection. I paused to look up at the traffic lights above my head, almost like I needed to see them to confirm that indeed I did finally reach this critical juncture. Then I turned to face my destination—Jamaica Station was only a couple blocks ahead. The street was filled with vehicles all similarly stuck in place. Everywhere I looked, traffic was at a complete standstill.

I passed a few pedestrians like me, searching for a way to get to their destinations. But the sidewalks were unusually empty; somehow, I expected it to be busier even though it was Christmas Eve and we were in the midst of one of the worst blizzards New York City had seen in decades.

By now my socks were thoroughly soaked. The chill was seeping into my feet and making them hurt, which then just made the rest of me feel cold and miserable.

You're going home to Jordan, I told myself. *All the suffering is worth it. Plus, you'll prove you're a good boyfriend.*

Just as true misery was starting to take root, despite my best efforts to keep it at bay, I found myself at the subway station. A smile crossed my lips as I took the stairs down.

That's where all the people were. Even before I could see them, I could hear them. I could feel the heat from them. When I reached the middle of the stairs, I found the crowd. There had to be hundreds, if not thousands, of people all crammed into the space.

A subway train came screeching into the station and the doors opened. The cars were already full with people from previous stations, yet some folks from here crammed themselves into the train. A few moments later, it pulled away. That hadn't even made a dent in the crowd.

I almost wondered if I should go back up to the surface and try walking home. It'd be cold and wet and very long, but it might actually get me there faster than I expected the trains to do. But as I looked behind me to give that thought more consideration, a wave of people came down the stairs, effectively blocking my exit, while moments later another train came screeching into the station. This one wasn't as full as the previous one, but it certainly wasn't empty. I'd estimate maybe a few dozen people packed themselves into the train before it finally pulled away.

As a result, the crowd did move forward enough for me to take a tiny step toward the platform. Sighing, I decided I was in this for the long haul. It was going to be tough, but it was better than braving the weather and risking frostbite or getting lost.

I just hoped Jordan wasn't worrying about me too much. By now he would know my flight had been cancelled and he wouldn't be able to reach me what with my lost phone.

If I were him, I'd be freaking out.

Chapter Five

Jordan

MANDY HAD BOUGHT THE SECOND round of hot chocolates.

We discovered the vending machine *did* offer whipped cream as an option—and for free—but after we both had it on our first drinks, we decided it was better off plain. The whipped cream was…well…obviously fake. It tasted like plastic.

Despite the topping tasting like a shopping bag, the rest of the hot chocolate was super good for a vending machine concoction. And after that first hot chocolate, we agreed not to talk about Benjamin and London. We would later, I was sure, but right now we needed to not mention them. This was about lifting ourselves out of depression, not digging a deeper hole to fall into.

As I finished my second cup, I leaned back in the chair. We'd found ourselves a cozy little sitting area next to a tall set of windows. It gave us a perfect view of the devastating snowstorm and the dark-as-night sky.

Somehow the two hot chocolates made it a not-so-depressing sight.

"We need to make tonight special," I said. I looked over at her; she was leaning back in her seat, similarly to me, but cradling her still half-full hot chocolate.

"Like how?" she asked. "It's just the two of us and a handful of random strangers somewhere in the building. And there are no Christmas decorations anywhere. It's a sterile dorm."

I didn't exactly know what we could do either. Sighing, I tried to come up with some sort of answer. Eventually, my thought process took me to the Rainbow Club. "Do you still have keys to the club room?" I asked.

She looked at me and blinked a few times, clearly confused. "Yeah."

"Do you think there's enough stuff in the kitchen there to make cookies?"

"Cookies? Maybe?" She seemed very uncertain.

"What?" She had a funny look on her face.

"I'm not much of a baker." She finished off her hot chocolate and put the cup next to mine. "London and I agreed that when we get our own apartment I will never cook. Trust me, I'm a disaster in the kitchen. Did you know it's possible for brownies to explode?"

I tried to keep a straight face, but failed. I snickered and then laughed, and soon Mandy was laughing along with me.

"Come on," I said, as I hooked my elbow in hers, "let's get baking!"

We went to our dorm rooms to grab our coats and

boots and for Mandy to get her keys, then we began the long journey to the Rainbow Club room. It was in a different building than our dorm, so we had to trudge through the snow outside, giving us our first real glimpse of just how bad the storm was. Just from crossing a small area to a nearby building, our heads and shoulders were covered in a thick dusting of snow and my hands and feet were already frozen. The occasional gust of biting, icy wind slammed into us and made my cheeks hurt. The side door we normally go through was locked, so we had to trudge around the building to the main entrance and, thankfully, it was open. We got inside and stomped our feet to knock off the snow. I shivered from the cold—and the fact the heat in this building was set super low, since it was mostly empty, certainly didn't help matters. I kept my coat zipped up tight as we proceeded through mostly-darkened corridors to the even-darker lower levels. By the time we got there, I had warmed up a bit and we were laughing—sharing stories of awkward Christmases. Like the one where I got food poisoning at my grandma's house and tried to hide it. People clued in something was wrong when I threw up into the potted plant in the living room.

Mandy slid her key in the lock and opened the door to the Rainbow Club. The club room beyond was pitch black. There were no windows down here, so it was blacker than night when the lights weren't on.

"It's almost kind of spooky right now," she said as she tiptoed in.

"Boo!" I shouted as I grabbed her shoulders.

She screamed and then turned around and hit

me...and then we both broke into laughter. A moment later she found the light switch and the room was bright and decidedly less spooky. The Rainbow Club was little more than a studio apartment—again without windows. There were a couple futons and a coffee table on one side, a tiny kitchen on the other, a door to a little closet, and another door to a cubicle of a washroom.

And, unexpectedly, there was a small artificial Christmas tree on the coffee table.

"Where'd this come from?" I asked Mandy as I walked up to the tree. It was no more than a foot and a half high and other than a rainbow ribbon wound around it like garland, it was bare of decorations.

Mandy's eyebrows pinched together as she looked at the tree. "I have no idea. And, like, it wasn't here yesterday when I locked up." She slowly turned in place, looking around like she was making sure nothing was missing.

"Other people have keys, though, right?" I said.

She just kind of shook her head as she continued looking around. "Yeah, but they both went home earlier in the week—I'm the only key holder left." When she completed her examination, she turned back to face me. "Nothing seems to be missing...so someone broke in to leave us a little Christmas tree?"

"Broke in...or it's Santa," I said as I winked at her.

She rolled her eyes. "Right. It was probably a custodian. Still strange, though." She shook her head again. "Anyway, cookies?"

"Oh yeah!" We threw our coats on the futon and I crossed the space to the kitchen. I dug through the cupboards and found flour, sugar, chocolate chips, and a few other ingredients. "The big test, of course, is the wet ingredients." I opened the little bar fridge, expecting to be disappointed. Weirdly, there were the remaining three ingredients right there—margarine, milk, and eggs. I quirked my eyebrow and looked over at Mandy.

"What?" she asked.

I pulled the ingredients out of the fridge. "I was expecting to have to improvise and cobble something together. Instead, we have everything we need." I opened the milk, expecting the pungent stench of rotten milk. That was not what I smelled. "And it's fresh too." I opened the carton of eggs. "And…eggs. I, uh, am very confused as to why this is here. Confused, but relieved."

"So…" Mandy said, "someone broke in to leave us a Christmas tree and all the ingredients we need for cookies?"

I shrugged. "Again, I offer Santa as a possible explanation."

She stuck her tongue out at me. "So, how do we make these cookies?"

As we set to the task of making a batch of cookies without an electric mixer or a full oven—we had a toaster oven—I couldn't help but reflect on the oddness of the Christmas tree and the all-too-perfect cookie ingredients. While I was obviously too old to believe in Santa, this stuff was weirdly unexplainable. While a custodian *could* have left the tree here, perhaps a queer custodian wanted to leave a surprise for the members, there really wasn't an explanation for the full set of cookie dough ingredients.

We managed to mix the dough decently well given we were using wooden spoons and some muscle power. We used a tablespoon to scoop out dollops of dough and drop it onto the toaster oven's little baking sheet.

With the first batch in the toaster oven—and given the tiny size of it, we would be doing *several* batches—we sat down on the futons. Between us was the coffee table and the mostly-bare Christmas tree.

I leaned forward and ran my fingers through the tips of the fake tree. "This needs decorations."

"Wait," Mandy said. She stood and hurried over to the little storage closet, quickly returning with a small pad of colored paper and a little tub of art supplies.

Together we cut out and decorated little ornaments and then used paper clips to hang them on the tree. This kept us busy through the seven batches of cookies. When the cookies were finally all done, so was the tree. For the tree topper, Mandy had done some sort of origami thing to make a somewhat-star-shaped topper, upon which I heaped lots of glue and glitter.

"It's perfect," she said.

"It is," I agreed. I didn't think I'd ever get the glitter off of my jeans, but it was worth it if it helped make this Christmas just a little bit more special.

I put all the cookies onto a large plate and then washed the tray and the bowl, leaving them in the dish rack to dry. While I did that, Mandy packed away the craft supplies. I picked up the plate of cookies and turned to Mandy. "Well, better head back, I guess." We put on our coats.

She looked at the tree. "It feels a shame to leave this here in the dark where no one will see it." She bit her lip. "We should take it."

"Take it…and put it where?" It seemed odd to take the tree that definitely wasn't ours—but also seemingly wasn't anyone else's given no one had a key.

"I don't know—the lounge?"

Our floor in our dorm building had a little communal lounge near the central stairwell. There were a couple overstuffed couches and overstuffed chairs and some heavily scratched tables. During the week it was often a highly-coveted study area and during the weekend it was usually a casual hangout spot.

"Sure, I guess." It still felt a little odd to take the tree, but I did agree with her it needed to be with people who would appreciate it.

She picked up the tree, and carefully put it in a plastic grocery bag, trying her best to not jostle the ornaments too much, and we headed out of the Rainbow Club and back through the snow-laden and wind-scoured "greenspace", eventually finding our way back to our building and our floor.

We went straight past our dorms to the lounge and Mandy put the tree in the middle of the coffee table at the center of the furniture.

"I have to admit it looks way better here. Way less depressing than an abandoned student club in the basement." I chuckled. "It also makes this place feel a little more like Christmas."

I put the plate of cookies down on the table next to the tree.

"All prepared for Santa," Mandy said. "We just need a glass of milk and a fireplace with stockings."

I laughed and then stuck my tongue out at her. "What happened to you rejecting my Santa hypothesis?"

"I never said Santa wouldn't come and eat the cookies," she said, "but I'm sure he wouldn't leave a tree and a carton of milk in some student lounge."

I rolled my eyes and then laughed. I plunked myself down on the couch and Mandy sat beside me.

"This Christmas won't be too awful after all," I said.

Mandy smiled at me. "It'll be pretty nice, I think."

Chapter Six

Benjamin

I FELT LIKE I WAS PRECARIOUSLY standing on the edge of the subway platform. I was fully behind the yellow line, but with the hundreds of people behind me forming an impassable wall of bodies, I felt claustrophobic, like they were pushing me forward, about to push me over the edge.

Calm down, Benjamin, I told myself. *What would Jordan tell you? Breathe. Just breathe.* I couldn't help but smile at that—normally it's me calming him down, me reminding him to breathe, but a situation like this would be the perfect opportunity for Jordan to turn the tables on that and be the one that was cool and calm and in control.

I had been here in the station for well over an hour now. It was probably going on two hours, if not more. I couldn't see the clock anymore, and even though I still instinctively reached into my pockets, I still didn't have my phone, so I couldn't be sure of the time. I probably would have been on the train a half hour ago if I hadn't been desperate to use the restroom. To use that meant going backward through the crowd until I reached the open door on the far wall. And when I came back out, it felt wrong to push my way back to the front, so I just took a new spot at the back of the crowd and went through a long wait again.

My feet ached and I was all sweaty and gross. With all these people packed in here and with the heat steadily flowing through the overhead vents, the ambient temperature had skyrocketed. I had my jacket open and I'd stuffed my hat into my backpack.

Damn, I was miserable. And who knew how long the journey was ahead of me. If I was super lucky, I could take the train all the way to Manhattan and just walk the few blocks home. I could be in Jordan's arms before I knew it. We'd be crammed in the subway car like sardines, but I could get through that if I kept Jordan in my mind as my end goal.

I could hear and feel the train before it arrived in the subway station. There was a screech coming from the darkness and a rush of air that, while smelling stale, felt glorious on my sweaty, overheated face. Following soon after, I saw the lights of the train and it whooshed into the station and screamed to a halt.

The doors opened—one of them was right in front of me—and the car was nearly full. Despite this, people on the train shuffled backward, cramming themselves in tighter to make room for more people. Around me, the crowd surged forward with one woman bumping me aside so she could get on the train.

Soon the car was full and there was no more room for

me. The train doors still stayed open, as if inviting more people aboard, but everyone around me just waited for the next one. I was ready to give up and just sit down on my suitcase and wait until everyone in New York City got to their destination before me so the trains would be blissfully empty. That might mean getting home sometime tomorrow, but it would be free of all this depressing hassle. I could find a coffee shop and wait several hours and come back and find this place empty. Of course, that might mean not getting home until December 26th and destroying any chance of a happy Christmas with Jordan.

"There's room for one more," came a voice. It was strong and clear and somehow I knew the voice and its words were intended for me.

I lifted my depressed head and saw a short woman in a hijab in front of me, standing just inside the train. She held out her hand for me.

"Let's get you home," she said, staring straight into my eyes. I felt captivated by that gaze in ways I couldn't quite comprehend.

I blinked at her several times; I was unable to process this moment of kindness in the hours of crushing defeat of standing in this subway station.

A crackle came through the train's speaker system, and a clearly exhausted voice said, "Please stand clear of the doors."

Acting on impulse, I took the woman's hand and stepped across the gap and into the train, pulling my suitcase behind me. As soon as I was inside, the doors slid closed.

I was inside the train. I was a giant step closer to Jordan.

For a moment, my knees almost felt weak, like I was overwhelmed by the fact that I was actually making progress, that I was actually going to spend Christmas with my boyfriend and not in some dirty, overheated, overcrowded subway station. I almost felt like crying—it was a weird and overpowering rush of emotions that were barreling through me.

The train juddered as it slowly moved forward, picking up speed with every passing second. I looked out the window and watched all the faces still on the platform. They looked exhausted, depressed and worn out. I knew if I could have seen myself on the platform, I would have looked the same. Now, though, I felt a new energy in me, like I'd tapped into a new source of strength deep inside. That rush of weird and overpowering emotions faded away and all that remained was confidence and joy. *I will make it home to Jordan for Christmas.*

"Thank you," I said, turning back to the woman in the hijab who had pulled me onto the train. But she was no longer standing in front of me. Instead, an older gentleman glanced up at me and then stared out the window, letting out a heavy sigh.

Where did she go?

She couldn't have gone far given how crammed this train car was. I scanned the crowd, looking for her, but saw no sign of her. It was almost like she never existed. Like it was magic or something.

"Benjamin?" a voice called out.

I turned around, searching for the source of that voice—for the person who apparently knew me. A waving hand pulled my attention to the right person.

"London?" I almost couldn't believe it—London and her girlfriend Mandy were good friends of ours from the Rainbow Club. Of all the possible people to run into on the subway today, London was both unexpected and a blessing. "I thought you went home already!"

She squeezed her way through the crowd, moving through half the subway car to get to me. The other passengers seemed exhausted and ambivalent about having to squeeze in tighter to accommodate her passing by. After a few apologies to people, she found her way right against me, pressed up tight like we were sardines.

London gave me a hug. God, it felt good. The only thing better than this right now would be a hug from Jordan. But a hug from London felt like I was halfway there.

"Aren't you supposed to be home by now?" I asked.

She nudged her glasses higher up her nose. She looked as exhausted as I felt. "I was supposed to," she said. "My flight was very early this morning, but it got delayed until mid-morning and, well…I'm sure you're on this subway for the same reason."

"Yeah. Sat on the tarmac for several hours until they just gave up and cancelled the flight." I paused and bit my lip, the feelings of today suddenly overwhelming me again. "And my phone got stolen or I lost it or something, so I haven't even had a chance to message Jordan. He probably thinks I'm being picked up at the airport back home by my parents now. He doesn't even know I'm still here, that I'm trying to get back to our dorms."

London put her hand on my elbow and gave it a squeeze. "Don't take this the wrong way, but now I don't feel so bad—I left my phone back in my dorm. Mandy doesn't know either. She's probably a little miffed by now that she hasn't heard from me. I was supposed to land a couple hours ago and then call her right away."

I thought back to Charlie in the cab. "Actually, I think the cell towers are down—Mandy might be cut off from calling home. She probably thinks you're there." I thought of Jordan and what he might be thinking right now. "Jordan is probably thinking the same, like this Christmas is one huge disaster and we're spending it in different states. He doesn't know I'm doing all I can to get back to him."

A crushing wave of sadness slammed into me. Not only was this the worst Christmas I've ever had—and this Herculean effort to get back to NYU certainly wasn't helping—but Jordan likely thought this was far worse. I *knew* I was in New York and trying to get to him; he probably thought I was having Christmas Eve dinner with our families and just ignoring the fact he wasn't with us.

London pulled me into a second hug. Though she was far shorter and slimmer than me, I melted into that hug. It was a human touch I so desperately needed right here and right now. The hug brought me strength and resolve. *I will get home to Jordan. I will make this Christmas special,* I told myself.

When we separated from our hug, I said, "What do you think Mandy and Jordan are doing right now?"

She shook her head and stared into the middle distance between us, thinking it through, then she looked up at me with sparkling eyes. "I just hope neither one of them attempted to get to the airport, otherwise they're stuck in this mess with us. If we're lucky, they never left the dorm and they're still there. I'm sure they're beyond depressed, but I hope they're not too devastated."

I sighed and leaned back against the metal pole right behind me. My backpack crunched with my weight pressed against it. I realized there were some gifts in there—the gifts were fine, but the little boxes they were in were probably crushed. Whatever. It wasn't like a crinkled box was going to ruin Christmas.

She leaned against the rail behind her too. The people around us were pressed in tight. The rest of the car seemed mostly silent, like we were the only ones talking. I took a look around and, yeah, almost everyone seemed to be depressed and staring into nothing. I couldn't blame them; they probably felt exactly like I felt, whether they lived here in the city or not.

"How long have you been with Jordan again?" she asked.

I smiled and then chuckled, partly at the fact this was the second time I was telling this story tonight, but also some residual embarrassment over my behavior in the early days with Jordan. "That's a little complicated. Our first kiss was almost a year ago—January first, to be exact—and we did some tentative dating, but some of my baggage got in the way and he dumped me. But at prom I made my final play for him and won his heart." I grinned and felt my cheeks warm with a blush; I looked down at my feet until I felt that blush soften. "Or to be more exact, I won my prince." I still remembered that moment like it was yesterday—after being crowned prom prince with Nikki as my prom princess, I stopped the dance, came out to everyone, declared my love for Jordan, and put my crown on his head as we danced in the center of the floor. Nikki got to do that dance with her boyfriend Winston. My coming out not only saved our relationship, but it seemed to help Nikki and Winston along too.

"You're such a softie," London said, lightly teasing me. She said things like this now and then because I defied the typical stereotypes of what a jock athlete would be like. A few weeks after we first met, she confided in me she was determined to not like me when we were introduced—she expected me to be as misogynistic and party-obsessed as all the other jocks she knew.

"Well, Jordan brings that out in me." I found myself staring at the tiny speck of floor between us again, waiting for another blush to recede.

The subway screeched to a halt as we came rushing into the next station. I swayed against the pole I was leaning against, but did my best not to bump into anyone else. The doors opened and revealed a station just as crammed with people as Jamaica Station was. I stepped sideways toward London, basically pressing our sides together, to make a little room for other people to cram in with us.

Indeed, some people did. As well, a few people pushed themselves through the crowd to get off at this station, freeing up a little more space. London and I moved further inward and at least a dozen people squeezed in through the door we were, just moments ago, almost pressed up against. If I felt like sardines before, I now felt like sardines with claustrophobia. It certainly didn't help that London and I both had backpacks and suitcases. We tried piling our luggage vertically between us and bracing our bodies around it, so that we hopefully took up less room.

A few minutes later, the doors chimed and slid closed and the subway pulled away from the station.

"Tell me about you and Mandy," I said. "How long have you been together?"

"Well," she said, and there was a slight blush on her cheeks. I was glad to not be the only blusher when talking about our partners. "We didn't really have the drama you two had. Mostly because she didn't know I existed."

"What?" I blurted out. "I can't see her ignoring you. She's too nice for that!"

She shook her head. "No, she didn't ignore me. I just pined from afar. I was a barista at Starbucks and she liked to hang out there with her friends to study for tests." She laughed and looked up at me, her cheeks still reddened. "It took me a *long* time to ask her for more than just her order..."

My heart skipped a beat when I saw her come in. It was like all the hustle and bustle of Starbucks went quiet whenever she entered. It was April and the snow was almost gone, but the ground was a mess of puddles and sloppy, dark snow. She stomped her shoes on the mat just inside the door.

And that was when she looked up at me and made eye contact with me. My heart skipped another beat. I quickly looked down at the espresso machine I was wiping down.

Ask her out, *a voice in my head said.* Do it already.

She'd been coming in for months now, always ordering a special drink and usually studying with a bunch of friends, but sometimes she was here by herself. I took a quick look around and couldn't see anybody I recognized as being part of her study group—either she was the first one of her group here or this was an alone day. Perfect time to ask her out, *that voice in my head said.*

I moved to the register as she came up to give me her order.

"Hi," she said.

"Hey," I managed to say. I was so nervous that there was a very real chance I'd vomit all over her shoes.

"Can I get a tall caramel macchiato?" she said. I loved the way those words spilled from her mouth.

"Sure," I said, punching in the order. "How would you like it?" She always had a modification or two. I looked up at her and our eyes locked and neither one of us spoke for a very long moment.

"Um..." she said, "yes. Can you add an extra shot of espresso and use soy milk instead?"

I glanced over my shoulder to verify my manager wasn't hovering again. "Sure," I said, but didn't punch it in so she wouldn't have to pay the upcharge. I was sure she noticed I was giving her a deal, because she smiled as she handed over the cash.

"Mandy, right?" I said as I wrote her name on the cup. I knew her name, of course. Every time I said or heard it, it made my heart go pitter-patter.

"Yeah," she said. "You're London, right?"

I smiled and shyly pointed at my nametag. "I guess it's obvious, right?"

She looked at the nametag and then back up at my eyes with a slight blush on her cheeks. The blush looked cute on her. "Oh, I knew already."

I blushed myself and focused on writing her name on her cup, not that I needed to. When she walked toward the other end of the bar to wait for her drink and I had a few moments of privacy, I wrote "Will you go out with me?" on the side of the cup and put my number underneath it, then covered it all up with a cardboard sleeve.

When I walked down to the end of the bar where the espresso machine was sitting, I found her watching me.

"I really like your hair up like that," she said. I had recently let it grow a little longer and instead of having it hang over my shoulders, I put it up in a loose, messy bun.

"Thank you," I said. It gave me the opening for giving her a compliment, something I've been wanting to do for a long time. "I really love your sweater."

She looked down at her sweater that peeked out from where her coat was unzipped. "Thank you." She suddenly sounded very shy as she said, "I was hoping you'd like it."

Oh my God, *I thought. I was suddenly thankful I had put my phone number on her cup because right now my brain was so muddled I didn't know if I'd get the number correct now.*

I quickly whipped up her drink and then slowly slid it across the counter toward her. Just before she grabbed it, I loosened my grip on the cup so the little cardboard sleeve fell down to the bottom of the cup, revealing my handwritten message for her.

Her eyes widened as she read the message and for one long horrible heartbeat I was worried I had misread the whole situation, but then she smiled and said, "I'll text you my number now."

"That would be awesome," I said.

Then she took her cup and sat at a table that gave us a very clear view of each other. She pulled out her phone and typed something into it. When my manager went into the back room, I discreetly pulled my phone out of my pocket and saw a message from her.

"...And that was around April or so," she said, finishing her story.

I laughed. "So, it's either longer or shorter than Jordan and I, depending on when you feel the actual start of my relationship is. Very smooth pick-up move, by the way." She winked in response.

I was again beyond glad I had run into London. While this day was still miserable, it was far less miserable than it would have otherwise been. I tried to imagine this subway ride without her—I'd be one of those passengers just depressed and staring at nothing, waiting for this day to be over. I mean, I was still waiting for this day to be over, but I wasn't as depressed as I otherwise would have been.

The subway squealed as it pulled into the next station. The doors opened to another platform crammed with people.

The speakers above the doors crackled to life and the train conductor's voice came through. "I'm sorry to make your Christmas Eve more difficult, folks, but ahead of us are numerous power failures and the lines are closed due to the storm. This is the end of the line for us. The last stop. Please disembark and find an alternate way to your destination. I apologize for the inconvenience and hope you're able to find some happiness and warmth tonight." The speakers crackled and then went dead.

Around us, hundreds of people, if not thousands, collectively groaned.

I swore under my breath.

"I guess we're walking the rest of the way," London said. We let the train car—and the platform—empty out a fair bit before we navigated, putting on our backpacks and dragging our suitcases behind us. Soon we were absorbed into the gray, depressed crowd.

Right now, even the presence of a friend couldn't save Christmas.

Chapter Seven

Jordan

KETTLE OBTAINED!" MANDY SHOUTED as she came speed-walking down the hallway toward the little lounge we were turning into our Christmas oasis. She still had snow on the shoulders of her coat and melted snow had created glistening droplets of water in her hair.

We had decided we wanted more hot chocolate but didn't want to pay for more of it from the vending machine. I knew my roommate had a box of hot chocolate packets stashed away in his desk and Mandy had gone in search of a kettle. We knew there was one in the Rainbow Club, and she lost rock-paper-scissors and had to be the one to trudge through that desolate winter wasteland between our building and the student center.

"Any luck?" she asked as she got nearer.

I had both my laptop open and my iPhone on, desperately in search of a signal. I just wanted to call home and wish everyone a merry Christmas, and maybe tell

Benjamin I loved him and that somehow we'd make up for missing our first Christmas together.

"Not one bit," I said with a heavy sigh. I shut my computer and turned off my phone. I was getting zero cell signal—no bars, not even a flicker of a bar—and my computer was able to connect to the university's wifi routers, but there was no actual internet available.

"I know what my dad would say to that," Mandy said. She sat down and searched around the couches for a plug.

I laughed. "I think all dads would say the same thing. Something like, 'When I was your age we didn't have internet or cell phones and we got by just fine.'"

"Dads like to remind their kids of things like that, even though they know we know it already." Mandy was still searching for that plug. She stood up and nudged the couch away from the wall, looking behind it.

"No outlets?" I asked.

She shook her head. When she turned to look at me, her gaze went past me and locked on something. I turned to see what she was looking at—a plug on the opposite wall, right next to the floor-to-ceiling windows that were adjacent to the stairwell.

"Wanna move the furniture?" I asked.

Together we moved all of the lounge furniture to the window. We arranged the couches and chairs in a semi-circle facing the window, with the coffee table at the center of it all and little end tables between the couches and chairs. As a finishing touch, we put our short Christmas tree on the coffee table, right in front of the window.

Mandy plugged in the kettle and I tore open two packets of hot chocolate mix and dumped them into two, mostly-clean, mugs I grabbed from my room. Then I kicked back in a seat, putting my feet up on the table.

"It's really coming down," I said. It looked like the snow hadn't lessened and the sky was still perpetually dark. It was early evening, though, so it was normally getting dark at this time. Those cars were still abandoned in the intersection below, only now covered with so much snow they didn't really resemble cars anymore.

"What's winter like where you're from?" Mandy asked. She similarly had her feet up on the table and was lounging quite comfortably.

"We get snow," I said, "but nowhere near this much." I chuckled. "Though it seems like New York doesn't usually get this much either."

"We get lots in North Dakota. I don't know if we've ever gotten this much in one day, but we get mountains of snow over the winter and it's sometimes not fully gone until May."

"May?" I said. "Wow! Ours is usually gone in March. Have you ever had a snowpocalypse like this?"

She craned her neck to see the ground several floors below. It was difficult to get a sense of how much deeper the snow had gotten since we were last outside, since there was no one out there for comparison. The sidewalks were empty and so were the streets, save for those snow-covered abandoned vehicles. The lights at the intersection still regularly rotated between green and yellow and red, but not a single car passed through.

"It's kind of hard to really tell," she said. "We probably haven't had as much as this in one day, but, yeah, we've had some pretty intense snowfalls. We're equipped to handle it, though, because it's a little bit normal for us there than it is for this city here."

A memory suddenly struck me. "We're the complete opposite. There was one year where we had two or three inches of snow overnight—which is a *lot* for us in one day—and school was almost cancelled."

"Yikes," Mandy said. "It takes a lot more snow than that for school to be cancelled in North Dakota."

The kettle suddenly clicked and turned itself off. She poured hot water into both of our mugs and stirred the hot chocolate with a stir stick. I took my mug from her, blew off some of the steam, and took a tentative first sip. It was sweet but also super hot and burned my lip a little bit.

Several long moments of contemplative silence settled over us. It was nice. It was peaceful and quiet and cozy—all of the things I wanted Christmas to be. The only thing missing was Benjamin. I hoped he was safely back home now and having fun roughhousing with his brothers. I had a little pang of sadness at not having him here, but with how the day had progressed with Mandy, missing Benjamin seemed to hurt less and less. I wouldn't get over missing him, but we could still make this an enjoyable Christmas. Mandy seemed to be doing similarly with her missing London.

"Jordan, tell me about you and Benjamin," Mandy said.

I looked at her for a moment before responding. "What do you want to know?"

"Anything. How you met or who asked who out first or whatever you want to tell me."

"Well," I said, and then trailed off, trying to think of something. "Benjamin and I grew up as neighbors; we could see each other's bedrooms from our windows. We used to hang out all the time and always slept over at each other's place. Around freshman year of high school, he suddenly put some distance between us. We were still loosely friends, but we definitely moved in different directions."

"Oh, I'm sorry," Mandy said. She took a sip of her hot chocolate.

I smiled and looked down at my mug as I cradled it in my lap. "No need to be sorry. I later found out freshman year was when he started realizing he had feelings for me and he didn't know what to do with them."

She blinked quickly a few times. "I thought you once said you came out first, and Benjamin came out way later."

I nodded. "Yup. I came out right before senior year. Benjamin had me believing he was straight that whole time. It wasn't until New Year's Eve—almost twelve months ago—that I found out the truth."

"What happened?"

I laughed and felt a blush warm my cheeks. "He, uh, kissed me at the stroke of midnight."

"Get out!" Mandy shouted and grabbed my forearm. "What was that like? Your straight former best friend suddenly kissing you?"

"It was, well, awkward. I think I froze or something and he thought I hated it." I took a sip of hot chocolate to give myself a moment to think of how to phrase the next part. "The next six months were a real roller coaster as we went from 'why is my straight friend kissing me?' to him declaring his love for me in front of the whole graduating class, but with us breaking up in between those two events."

She guffawed. "How did I not know all this?"

I winced. "I think it sometimes embarrasses Benjamin to talk about how he effed up the whole trying to date me thing—like, it was really rough at times—so we don't usually tell people all the details. Maybe I shouldn't have said all this…"

She put her hand on my forearm. "Hey, I understand. This is just between you and me."

"Thanks," I said. I still felt kind of bad for blabbing all I did, even though I still left out some of the more difficult periods we went through. To distract myself, and to give myself a little burst of sugar to feel better, I grabbed one of the cookies off the plate and bit into it. "God, these are delicious." I shoved the rest of it in my mouth and swallowed, then said, "Tell me about you and London."

Mandy put a hand over her face and around it I could see her reddening cheeks. Then she cleared her throat and used both hands to cradle her hot chocolate mug and take a deep sip. "Well, our versions of events are different. She'll tell you she was a barista and I was always studying in her coffee shop and it took her a long time to work up the courage to ask me out. But…"

"But? Oh, I think I'm gonna like this."

"But...the reason I kept showing up there to study was so I could work up the courage to ask *her* out. I was a nervous, sweaty wreck every time I went into her Starbucks and I was going broke buying special drinks. I don't even really like lattes! The only reason I bought all the fancy stuff is because it gave me an excuse to talk to her a little longer because she would ask questions about how I want my drink." She laughed at her memories. "There was even a stretch where I had no homework or studying to do, but I was desperate to see her so I started re-doing assignments. I aced all my classes but I couldn't say more to her than a coffee order. It was finally her that scrounged up the courage to make the first move. If she didn't do that, I'd probably still be there re-doing assignments."

I giggled thinking of Mandy—and London—being so nervous and flustered. I knew them both as outgoing people who did whatever they wanted. To think of them both as being so painfully shy just didn't compute.

My giggling was suddenly interrupted by a very loud rumble from my stomach. I realized then I was famished.

"What time is it?" I asked. "I haven't really eaten since breakfast."

Mandy pulled out her phone—I could see, even from here, she still had zero bars. "It's going on eight o'clock. I think there was a cafeteria open, but only till six or something."

"Damn, and I bet no one's delivering now—not that we can even call anybody. I guess it's vending machine sandwiches for Christmas Eve dinner?" I wasn't as down about that as I expected. Hours ago, that dinner option would have felt devastating. Now, it felt kind of fun.

"I'll treat," she said with a wink. "It'll be my Christmas present to you."

Chapter Eight

Benjamin

I STILL DON'T KNOW WHERE ALL THOSE hundreds—maybe thousands—of people from the subway all went. It seemed we went up the stairs and spilled out onto the snowy sidewalk and everyone just sort of disappeared. Some walked away, hiking through the snow and soon fading away behind all the falling snow. A few went into the coffee shop across the street. There were definitely some who were hanging back in the station for warmth, or perhaps to wait to see if the subway would start up again in an hour or two. And still others were desperately trying their phones to call for friends or family with trucks to come rescue them, but from their angry and disappointed faces I knew they weren't getting through. But for all those people and all those options, the crowd thinned out surprisingly fast.

"Are you sure you know where we're going?" I asked London. I had my hat pulled down low on my forehead and I had my shoulders hunched up near my ears for extra warmth.

"Definitely!" she reassured me. "I've done this walk a few times in the fall, I know the route."

It felt like we had been walking for hours, trudging through the shin-deep snow, but I knew it was maybe a half hour or less. Every step took a ton of effort because the snow was so wet and heavy and clung to my shoes and the bottoms of my jeans. My feet were cold and frozen and starting to hurt.

I heard a deep rumbling behind me. Turning around, I saw a snowplow heading along the street in our direction. I stood and watched as it passed us by. Following along behind it was a caravan of vehicles, almost bumper-to-bumper, moving at the crawling pace of the plow.

Seeing all that made me think of Charlie. "I tried taking a cab back from the airport," I said as London and I continued our trek through the snow.

She scoffed. "Did you even make it very far?"

I shook my head, but when I realized she was in front of me and couldn't see me, I said, "Not really. We got stuck in the snow pretty quick, so I made my way to the subway."

She waved a mittened hand toward the road beside us, still with that endless caravan of cars slowly rolling down the street, and said, "Looks like you could get somewhere now. I mean, if you only wanted this street and none others and only if you're going in this direction."

I chuckled. "Even if the cab was right here, given how

today has gone, I don't think I'd be so lucky. We'd only get so far before we'd be stuck again."

We fell into silence as we trudged through another block. Even though the only traffic was the stream of cars beside us going in one direction, we waited until the light at the intersection turned green and allowed us to cross. When we reached the other side, we found ourselves beside a coffee shop.

"Warm up stop?" London asked.

"God, yes. My feet are frozen." Almost as if for show, my body decided to enter into a deep shiver, sending my teeth clattering.

London laughed in sympathy. "I wanted to make some smug comment about us North Dakotans being better prepared for the winter, but I'm effing freezing." She grabbed my bicep and pulled me through the doors.

Surely, on any other Christmas Eve, coffee shops like this were probably a dead zone with everyone home with their families. Any other Christmas Eve, they might even be closed at this time. Tonight, though, it was where dozens of stranded New Yorkers were waiting out the storm. Not only that…where I expected everyone to be miserable like us and like everyone back on that subway, the coffee shop was instead full of Christmas cheer. Indeed, when we entered, half the patrons looked up at us and most of them gave us smiles and a few of them even raised their coffee cups in hello. I turned to look at London with a raised eyebrow and she gave me a similar look back.

"Come on," I muttered, and led the way through the crowded coffee shop to the till.

"Hey," I said to the young woman at the register. "Can I get a coffee or something?"

She smiled. "You're in luck—coffee is free tonight. Call it a Christmas gift from management."

"Ooo, can I get a coffee too?" London said.

The barista nodded. "Anything else?"

I couldn't help but eye the pastry display. "Wanna share a bagel?" I asked London.

Her eyes lit up. I think she was as hungry as me. "Yes, please!"

"And a bagel," I told her, "warmed up and with butter, please."

She entered it in the register and I paid. A moment later we were both handed steaming cups of coffee that almost burned my hands when I took it from her, but it was an oh-so-good burn. It was the kind of burn where I could feel the warmth surging from my fingers to my hands and up to my forearms. I started to feel more like a human and less like an icicle.

London and I took our coffees to the station off to the side to pour in some milk and sugar. Just as we were searching for a spot to sit, the barista called us over for the bagel. Food and drink in hand, we stood at the edge of the sea of people, searching for a place to settle down. Unfortunately, all the seats were taken.

A waving hand caught my eye. There was a counter along the window at about mid-chest height with people standing alongside it, chatting with each other. One of the men at the end of the counter was waving us over.

I glanced at London. "Know him?"

"No. You?"

"Nope." I looked at the man again; he waved us over again. "I guess we get to make a new friend?"

London nodded and so I led the way through the mass of tables and people, coming up to the counter and the friendly-looking man standing there. He was with two other people—two women—and they all seemed happy to see us.

"You looked like you needed some friends," he said.

"I guess we could," London said. She extended her hand, introducing herself. After she did that, I stuck out my hand and did the same. The man who had called us over was Simon and his friends were a married couple he met here at the coffee shop in the same way he met us—he waved them over. Their names were Abby and Sarah.

I watched Simon as he told us the story of how he had ended up here at the coffee shop; he was clean-cut and clean-shaven with a head of close-cropped blond hair. He appeared to be a few years older than me, but not much more than that. He'd been let out of work early and knew the subway was going to be a disaster, so he put on his heavy boots and went hiking through the snow. He came in here for a warm-up almost two hours ago and didn't want to head back out into the storm yet.

"Besides," Simon said, "my husband is working until ten, so I would just be going back to an empty apartment. I'd much rather be here."

I blinked several times and sort of tilted my head. *Simon. Husband.* Things were coming together like puzzle pieces. "Is your husband Charlie? A cab driver?" I asked.

Simon's eyes opened wide and the grin that was already on his face only broadened. "Do you know him?"

I laughed. "I do! He picked me up at the airport and tried to get me home to my boyfriend, but we ended up getting stuck in traffic and stuck in snow." Simon's eyes seemed to beam with happiness when I told him about my very short in distance, but long in time, cab ride with Charlie. "He's really nice. And he told me all about you and how you guys started seeing each other."

Simon guffawed and covered his mouth with his hand. "He told you about the volleyball trip?"

"Sounded fun," I said with a wink.

Simon laughed again and covered his face with his hands. "I don't know if I want to ask what he said about me."

I took a bite of my bagel. "I keep my secrets. Driver and passenger confidentiality and all that."

Simon laughed, then said, "If I know my husband as well as I think I do, I know what he told you. He probably said something about how he was a nervous wreck and I was the cool, suave one. That is *not* how I remember it..."

I'd figured out I was bi like a few months before the volleyball tournament. And I knew what my feelings were because I was majorly crushing on Charlie. So, when we were assigned roommates for the tournament, I mentally jumped for joy when I saw I was with him.

I was pretty sure he was gay or bi too, but didn't know how to ask him. I didn't know how to make my move, either, because some of the other guys on the team were real douchebags and I knew if I read the situation wrong and Charlie was straight, then I'd be in for some major hazing and bullying.

I spent our whole first evening trying to work up the courage to talk to him, to ask him those questions I so badly wanted to ask him. But every time I thought I had an opening, my nerves got the better of me.

So, when we were watching TV and I stumbled on an episode of Queer as Folk, *I knew I had my opening. I'd been secretly watching the show without my parents knowing; I wasn't ready to come out to them and them knowing I was watching a gay show would certainly prompt them to ask those questions. But it was the opportunity I needed to finally speak to Charlie.*

I tried asking him about the show—there was a kissing scene on, I remember that clearly—but he wasn't giving me the opening I needed to be more direct with him. I could tell he wanted to have that conversation too but he was too scared.

Finally, I just flat out told him I'm bi.

And then he said he was too.

I was such a nervous wreck, but despite also being a bit nervous, Charlie was like the solid rock I could cling to.

After the tournament, when we were back at school, we were caught holding hands and soon everyone in the school knew. Someone wrote "fag" on my locker with a Sharpie. I was devastated my former friends could turn on me like that. My parents found out what was going on and they weren't really supportive. They figured it was just a phase and I'd grow out of it soon enough and find a woman and get married. I sometimes wondered if they were right, but then I pictured my life without Charlie and that was a life I didn't want.

The only *thing that kept me going was Charlie. I would not have survived the rest of high school without him.*

"I bet he told you it was *me* that was the rock *he* needed to get through that homophobia," Simon said. "I've heard him tell people that before. But it's totally not how I remember it. Charlie was the rock, the one steady, the stable point in a stormy and unpredictable sea."

I couldn't help but smile as Simon told me how much Charlie meant to him. They were a couple that was clearly in love and clearly meant to be together.

Reflecting on the two stories I'd heard, I couldn't help but notice they'd both had self-doubts about what they brought to their relationship, but they both felt the other person was the strong one in the relationship. Charlie had nothing but overwhelmingly positive things to say about Simon and Simon had nothing but overwhelmingly positive things to say about Charlie.

Simon and Charlie seemed like such a perfect couple, so loving and closely connected. I hoped when Jordan and I get a little older and get married we're like Charlie and Simon.

From there, our conversation turned to all of our relationships, with London and I telling them about Mandy and Jordan.

With Simon being the natural conversationalist that he was—and I got the sense he made a perfect party host—he brought Abby and Sarah into the conversation. And since all of our stories so far had been about our partners and how we met them, Simon said, "Tell us your story—we need to hear it."

Abby and Sarah looked at each other and shared a giggle from a shared secret. Like Simon and Charlie, Abby and Sarah only seemed to be a few years older than us. I glanced at London and saw her watching them with rapt attention and admiration; I realized she was probably thinking similar thoughts as I was. She likely was looking up to Abby and Sarah as a model of what she and Mandy could be like when they're further along in their relationship.

While keeping their gazes locked with each other, Abby said, "We were in a writers' group at university, one of those ones where you write a story and everyone reads it and offers feedback. I had no idea if Sarah was into women or if she was into me and I was just too shy to say anything. So, I wrote it into my stories…"

This was stupid. What if she thinks I'm gross for doing this?

Still, I couldn't stop. I scrolled through the stories on my computer, still debating on whether or not I should hit the "send" button on the email. It wasn't too late to back out, to tell the writing group the week got so incredibly busy I didn't have time to do any writing and had nothing to submit to the group. Or I could just pull up some old stuff I haven't sent around to the group yet.

"No," I told myself. I was alone in my dorm room, so it

was okay to talk to myself. Talking to myself was how I got through tough decisions. "I like her and I'm sure she likes me too. And if I can't screw up the courage to ask her out, then I have to let her know my feelings somehow."

I chewed my bottom lip as I scrolled through the next story. Would she figure it out? It was a lesbian romance short story and I wrote us into the story as characters. They weren't named after us, of course, but in every other way they were clearly her and I. This story was about a first date. The other two stories I was planning to submit were sequels to this one, showing the two characters continuing to date and their relationship growing.

"Screw it," I said, and hit the send button. My heart seemed to lurch as I realized there was no backing down. If she wasn't into me, then hopefully she was oblivious to what I'd done.

Sarah picked up the thread and continued…

I got a little excited when Abby's email appeared in my inbox. I loved her stories—every single one of them. She usually had a lesbian romance theme to her stories, which gave me an insight into her heart and I got to know her a little better through reading her stories.

Though I didn't understand it at the time, learning about her through her stories was making me fall in love with her.

The three stories she sent were so sweet, about two women our age finally working up the courage to ask each other out and go on a series of dates. It was when I reached the third story that I clued in the characters were very familiar. I mean, they had fairly generic names that were different than ours—but the women were clearly described as Abby and I, right down to my favorite pair of shoes.

I started sweating nervously. Not because I was upset by this, but because I didn't know how to move forward with this. Was this actually happening? Or was I just reading what I wanted to read into it? Like, was my head making this stuff up?

I wrote Abby an email and said I loved the characters, that they sounded like people I knew. But I asked her to change the characters' names.

Ten minutes later she sent the stories to me again with the characters now named Abby and Sarah. And she wrote a quick new scene where Abby nervously asks Sarah out on a first date for a coffee.

Abby jumped in, "And I asked her for feedback—should Sarah accept Abby's invitation for coffee or not?"

Sarah leaned over and kissed Abby. "I said yes, of course. And the rest is history. We got married two months ago."

"Congratulations!" London said. Then she asked to see the rings and the three women fawned over them.

I stepped closer to Simon and in a lower voice, asked him, "How did you know it was the right time to ask Charlie to marry you?" My heart thudded in my chest. While I was nowhere near ready to ask Jordan such a thing, it was a thought that popped into my head now and then. We often talked about our future together—our little house with our cats and dogs and cozy living room.

"It was Charlie that asked me," he said. "Still, I think you just know. One day you'll wake up and realize the time is right to ask."

I felt a blush warm my cheeks and I nodded. "Thanks."

"Are you thinking of asking Jordan?"

"One day," I said, honestly. "Not yet. Probably not while we're at university. But one day."

Simon put his arm over my shoulders. "Good man. Wait until the time is right. But whatever happens, whether you two get married or not, the only important thing is that you love each other."

"And I *do* love him. And he loves me."

"Good." Simon gave my shoulders a squeeze in a little side-hug.

Chapter Nine

Jordan

FOR A CHRISTMAS LACKING IN FAMILY and friends and all sort of Christmas busyness, tonight was actually turning out to be quite all right. I mean, other than the part about not having Benjamin here. My heart still ached whenever I thought of his absence, but each time it hurt a little bit less. Besides, New Year's Eve was the anniversary of our first kiss, so now I could focus all of this Christmas energy into that day instead and make it even more extra special.

For now, though, I could just enjoy Christmas Eve with Mandy. We'd finished our gourmet dinner a while ago of stale ham sandwiches from the vending machines by the cafeteria. After that we spent some time just watching the snow fall and pile even higher. It looked like it might be thinning out a bit, but with it now being into the full depths of nighttime, it was hard to tell. Were the clouds thinning? We had no way to really know.

About an hour ago, snow plows came through the

intersection down below, steering clear of the stalled cars. Traffic was almost non-existent, though. We saw a few vehicles pass through, moving at what had to be slower than walking speed, so there was some life outside of this dorm building. Still, it wasn't like things were back to normal. We still had no internet and no cell signal—we had no way to check if flights were on again at the airport and no way to call for a cab to get us there if we could catch flights. No, we'd accepted the fact we were spending Christmas together here in the university dorm.

And now we were talking about Benjamin and London again. It seemed to be our favorite topic.

"But when did *you* realize you had feelings for Benjamin?" Mandy asked. "I mean, you'd thought of him as your straight friend for all that time, right?"

I laughed and laid my head on the top of the couch back so I was staring up at the ceiling. We'd found where the light switches were and found we could turn off half the lights. It wasn't so blaringly bright in here anymore.

"I don't even really know when it happened," I confessed. "I started to develop some feelings for him before he kissed me and I knew his secret. Like, months before. But I brushed it aside because he was straight." I rolled my head to the side and looked at her. "I guess it would have to be sometime after that first kiss. It was after the kiss I clued in this could actually be a thing, that Benjamin and I could be a thing, that my feelings for him weren't quite so unrequited."

She grinned at me. "I love a good love story."

"We had our rocky parts," I told her. For some reason

I felt the need to make it clear we weren't perfect. Call it self-deflection, I guess.

"All the best love stories have rocky parts," she said. "What's important is how you get through those rocky parts."

I looked out at the snow again. The path that had been cleared by the plow looked pretty snowed over again. Maybe it wasn't lightening up.

"Rough parts like our first Christmas being in separate states?" I asked with a smirk.

"Exactly." She laughed. "Do you want to watch a movie or something? I've got a few saved on a hard drive so we don't need internet."

"Sure," I said.

She headed off to her dorm to retrieve what she needed. While I waited, I put my feet up on the coffee table, next to the little Christmas tree. On the other side of the tree sat the plate of cookies. We'd had a few of them, but there were still tons left.

While I had made my peace with how Christmas had turned out, I hoped we'd have internet again by the morning. I needed to see Benjamin. If I couldn't hold him, I wanted to hear his voice. It might be corny, but I wanted to kiss his image on my computer if I couldn't kiss him in person.

In a weird way, I almost wished Benjamin and I had both been trapped here at university together. It was kind of nice not being around the chaos of my family. And given this year we were going to combine his family and mine, the chaos would have been doubled. It would have been loud and stressful. Though our families had known each other forever, everything had kind of changed when Benjamin and I got together. We were no longer just friendly neighbors, but now we were like family. There would have been a lot of expectations placed upon us at Christmas dinner, or at least Benjamin would feel that way, especially if his Aunt Janine showed up. He worried a lot, perhaps too much, about how other people perceived him as my boyfriend.

I almost felt sorry for Benjamin for him being alone with both our families. He'd have so many people telling him they were so sorry I couldn't make it. He'd get frustrated with all of that and it would just add to everything going on in his head. I hoped he was at least able to get over any heartache for not having me there; I wanted him to just relax and be himself. If I was able to get over it, I hoped he would too, otherwise I worried I might feel guilty over it all. Already, I had a little pang in my gut of guilt—here I was enjoying my Christmas with Benjamin almost as an afterthought, while he might be devastated we can't be together on our first Christmas.

I must have made a grimace on my face because when Mandy came back with her laptop and a few other things, she said, "What's wrong?"

I shook my head, not wanting to get into it, but she made it clear she wasn't going to take no for an answer. "I was just thinking of Benjamin again. Feeling a bit guilty I'm having a good time without him. I mean, I miss him, but I'm having a great time here with you."

She put her computer down on the table and sat next

to me, putting a hand on my knee. "I get it. I think the same thing about me and London. But then I remind myself that London would want me to make the most of it and have as good a time as I could. I'm sure Benjamin would want the same for you."

I nodded. "You're right. I mean, he'd probably make me feel silly for moping all through Christmas over missing him. Making the best of it is what he'd want me to do."

"So," she said, holding up her laptop, "that means zombie movies for Christmas Eve!"

"Zombie movies?" I stared at her with disbelief. "Celebrate the magic of Christmas Eve with watching some gory movie?" I generally didn't do well with blood and gore. When Benjamin and I watched horror movies, I tended to bury my face in his chest so I didn't have to see what was on the screen. Of course, the upside to that was my face was buried in his chest.

I don't think Mandy would want me burying my face in her chest. I didn't really want that either.

"Do you have anything less..." I said, "I don't know...less Halloween and more Christmas?"

Her gaze drifted to the side, a tic I learned meant she was thinking. When her gaze snapped back to me, she said, "*Die Hard*?"

I blinked at her. "I was thinking, like, *The Grinch* or something."

"*Die Hard* is a Christmas movie," she said. "The whole thing takes place during an office Christmas party."

When I gave her another skeptical look, she asked, "Have you seen it?"

I shook my head. "Is it that good?"

"Oh my God it's fantastic and we're watching it right now!" She didn't wait for me to agree or disagree, she just booted up her laptop and plugged it in, then set us up with the movie. While she fiddled with the last few things, I went to the end of the hall and turned out the rest of the lights, plunging us into darkness, save for the emergency exit signs and the ambient light from outside reflecting off the snow and bouncing into here.

When I got back to the couch, the movie was starting up. I grabbed a cookie, sat back, and settled in. It was a good movie—better than I expected honestly, though calling it a Christmas movie might've been a little bit of a stretch. I yawned as the final credits rolled.

"God, what time is it?" I asked.

"After eleven," Mandy said as she closed her computer. She arched an eyebrow at me. "Do you really get that tired this early?"

"Well," I said, suddenly feeling awkward. "Um, with my roommate gone, Benjamin might've spent the night with me last night."

She held up her hands. "That's enough," she said. "I really don't want to hear more."

"London didn't spend the night with you?" I asked, projecting my unease fully onto her with an evil grin.

"I didn't say that. I just don't need to hear that detail about you and Benjamin."

I laughed evilly. "So, yeah, I'm tired. I don't know if I want to go back to my empty dorm room, though."

"I know what you mean." She looked around the set-up we had. "Do you want to sleep out here tonight? There are two couches, after all."

I looked up and down the corridor. We hadn't seen anyone for hours. Besides, it wasn't *that* unusual to see someone sleeping here in the lounge area—I often found guys out here on Saturday and Sunday mornings, likely passed out from a party the night before.

"Sure," I said. It would be good to have some company for the night and to have someone to wake up to on Christmas morning. I mean, it wouldn't be the same as waking up at home and finding a tree loaded with presents underneath and it wouldn't be the same as waking up with Benjamin, but it was something that would nonetheless make Christmas morning just a little bit more special.

I stood up. "I'll grab my blanket. Why don't you grab yours and stash your laptop. Meet you back here in ten?"

"Deal," she said.

I went to my dorm room and grabbed my blanket and pillow and made my way back to the lounge. After putting my makeshift bed together, I pulled out my phone again—still no cell signal and no internet. That didn't really surprise me; I had more or less accepted this Christmas was going to happen on its own schedule and things were going to happen in their own way and I had no control over any of it. I'd be thrilled when I had a connection again and could call or Skype home and wish everyone a merry Christmas and give lots of internet kisses to

Benjamin, but until that connection was possible, I was happy to let things stay the way they were.

"Any luck?" Mandy asked as she returned with her own blanket and pillow.

I put my phone down on the table next to the tree. "Nope. Still no signal."

"Meh," she said. "Sucks, but we'll live."

"We will," I agreed.

I watched her spread the blanket over her couch and then get into her makeshift bed. I laid my head on my pillow and pulled my blanket up to my shoulders. Our feet were facing the window and between us was the coffee table with the tree.

"Merry Christmas, Mandy," I said.

"Merry Christmas, Jordan," she said.

"Though this isn't what either of us wanted, I had a really great time with you today."

She smiled. "Thank you. I really enjoyed our day together. I'm looking forward to tomorrow."

"Goodnight," I said.

"Goodnight."

After a few moments, I rolled over and closed my eyes. And a few moments after that, I was drifting off to sleep.

I dreamed of Benjamin. Of having him in my arms. Of him cuddling here with me. Of us kissing under the mistletoe. Of us building a future together.

I'm sure I slept with a smile on my face.

Chapter Ten

Benjamin

MY FEET WERE SO COLD AND WET they were hurting again. But I needed to do this, I needed to trudge forward and make my way to Manhattan and then back to NYU.

London and I had stayed maybe a little too long at that coffee shop, but the atmosphere was so cozy and welcoming and we had such a good conversation going with Simon and Abby and Sarah that it was weirdly hard to pull ourselves away. And I don't know about London, but I felt like I learned a little bit tonight—like not only did I have a little glimpse of what the future could be like for Jordan and I as a gay couple, but through meeting Charlie and Simon and Abby and Sarah, I came to understand all couples were different. They each had their quirks. They each had their stories. They each had their way of existing as a couple.

If anything, this trek through New York City on Christmas Eve, hearing the stories I did and meeting the people I came across, was like a Christmas gift from the universe to me. I loved Jordan since we were kids and will continue loving him as long as he will love me back; I think tonight's journey helped me see love is really all we need. We didn't need to be a perfect couple. We didn't need to be like those gay couples we see on TV. No, we just needed to be true to ourselves and just love each other.

And right now I wanted to give Jordan all the loving I could give him.

"Can you slow down a little bit?" London called from behind me.

I paused and looked behind me. London was several yards back, struggling to keep up with me. Her face was flushed and she looked sweaty and hot—which I'm sure is how I looked given how my shirt was damp with sweat—and big clouds of fog erupted in front of her face every time she let out a heavy breath.

"Sorry," I said. "I think I'm just a little excited to be getting home to Jordan."

"I know," she said, as she caught up to me. We walked side-by-side for a bit. I'd long given up on trying to drag my suitcase; instead, I carried it beside me. My arms and shoulders ached from carrying this weight all day and evening. "We've still got miles to go, you know."

"Yeah, I know." We still had to walk across a bridge to Manhattan, never mind navigating Manhattan itself. Home never felt so far away, despite it physically being so close. If this were a hot and dry summer day, we would have long reached home. If the subway were working perfectly, we would have been home even sooner.

When we reached an intersection, London put her suitcase down and sat on it. I did the same. We'd been doing these little breaks every couple of blocks.

"How you doing?" I asked.

Despite looking hot and sweaty, she hugged herself and shivered. "I've been better," she said. "The worst part is my hands and my feet—I don't know if they'll ever be warm again."

I flexed my fingers in my mittens; they ached and felt slightly numb. "I know what you mean." I didn't need to flex my toes or rotate my ankles to know how sore my feet were.

I exhaled and was surrounded by a cloud of fog. When I looked up and down the two streets that made up this intersection, I found them almost completely empty. There was one person several blocks down crossing the street. Given the ridges of snow, a plow had come by some time ago, but the street had quickly been covered in a new blanket of snow. The storm was definitely slowing down, but the city was still almost impassable for traffic. A while back we had passed a subway station and on a whim we went down to see if it was up and running again—but it was one of the stations that was out of power. Only a couple emergency lights were on. So, we were stuck having to continue our walk through the city.

I looked down the street again and a lit-up sign caught my attention. It was one of those signs that had a strip across the bottom that flashed the temperature and the time.

"It's after midnight," I said when the 12:16 flashed below the store name. "Merry Christmas, London."

"Merry Christmas, Benjamin," she said.

I stood and stepped over to her, my arms outstretched. We hugged. This wasn't Jordan, but this was a friend. It felt good.

When we parted from the hug, I said, "What do you say we get moving again? Get home to where we belong?"

"I like the sound of that." London stood and picked up her suitcase. I followed her across the street as we stumbled through the deep ridges of snow the plow had left. As we continued walking, I'd hoped we'd find another coffee shop that was open. I just needed to warm up my feet and hands a little bit—sitting in a warm shop and cradling a cup of coffee would just about do it.

My heart almost skipped a beat when I saw the lit-up Dunkin' Donuts sign ahead of us, but when we reached it, the place was closed and the lights were out. My feet decided to ache just a little bit more at that moment, to remind me of the predicament I was in. I had to get home and I had to walk, there was no other option. And there was no way to warm up before then. I'd be lucky if I didn't get frostbite.

I don't know how long we were walking and I had no idea what time it was now, but we eventually reached a bridge. I was too tired and too exhausted to even know which bridge it was and where we were. All I knew was we had to walk across it and then traverse through Manhattan. We were a giant step closer, but we still had an incredibly long way to go.

"Can we rest a moment?" I asked. London nodded and stopped. I sat on my suitcase.

Everything felt so overwhelming. My painfully cold and wet feet. My exhausted legs and arms and shoulders. My overheated torso and head. The hours and hours I'd spent outside in the brutal cold. The miles and miles we'd walked and the many more miles we had to still walk.

I put my elbows on my knees and my face in my hands. I was almost ready to cry. Why did this have to be so hard?

I felt a hand on my shoulder. "Benjamin? Are you okay?"

I rubbed my face and sat upright. "I will be. I'm just…tired, I guess."

"I get it," London said. "The only thing that's keeping me going is knowing I can talk Mandy into a foot massage."

"Oh, a foot massage sounds nice," I said. "I think we both deserve one after all this."

"Foot massage…and hot water bottles and blankets," she said. She sort of stared into space, like she was already imagining it.

"And dry clothes," I added.

"Yes! And warm air that doesn't hurt your face."

"Mmm…" I could almost feel all of that. But then the illusion shattered and fell away when my cold and sore feet started throbbing and demanding attention. I swore and tried flexing my toes—the movement hurt, but I could feel a little bit of blood rushing to the area and warming them up just a little bit. I hissed through my teeth as sharp pain followed that warmth. *I'm definitely demanding a foot massage.*

"I guess we should continue on," London said.

I nodded and stood up. My muscles were so sore and tense, I felt like such an old man as I stood up and tried to pick up my suitcase. Damn, I was exhausted. I stared ahead of us. We were in the middle of the street now, no longer on the sidewalk—the snow was just easier to traverse here and there were no vehicles. Even so, the bridge was daunting. It was so long and so piled up with snow.

"Do you think we're going to make it?" I asked London. "Like, before we turn into icicles ourselves?"

London looked like she was trying to give me a humoring laugh but couldn't actually do it. "I wonder if we should have stayed at the airport."

"It would have been warm."

"They had restaurants."

I sighed. "I don't know if I have the strength to make it all the way back. I mean, *I will*, but I'm pretty much tapped out for energy right now, and I might be getting frostbite on my toes."

A tear gathered in the corner of London's eye and rolled down her cheek. "I know."

I pulled her into a hug again and I felt her let out a shuddered breath. I wanted to cry again, more than before. Though we had come so far, the path ahead just seemed so incredibly daunting.

We just stood there, hugging in the silent, cold night.

A faint rumbling sound penetrated that silence. The

sound grew louder and then a few moments later a bright light shone on us.

London and I broke from our hug and I stared straight into the light, trying to figure out what it was. It was a vehicle, obviously, and a large one.

A door slammed and then a man came in front of the vehicle, his form backlit by the powerful headlights. As he drew closer, I saw he was an older man—though I couldn't even begin to guess at his age because he somehow seemed timeless—and he had a big white beard that hung over his round belly. If I didn't know any better, I'd say he almost looked like Santa.

"You kids need some help?"

I looked at London before answering and she looked at me. I could read the silent message in her eyes. We needed to trust this man.

"We're trying to get home to NYU," I said. "We've been walking for hours now."

The man let out a laugh that shook his belly. "You really chose the wrong night for a walk. Hop on in; I'll take you home."

Relief instantly flooded through me, warming me. I grabbed both my suitcase and London's and followed the man to the passenger side of the vehicle. Now that the bright headlights weren't blinding me, I could see it was a huge truck, with the back of it piled with snow. It seemed he was part of the street clearing teams.

"I hope you don't mind dogs," he said as he opened the passenger door, which I noticed had the name *North Pole Trucking* painted on the side. The friendliest golden retriever I'd ever seen popped his head forward and sniffed my face. "His name is Rudy."

I put a suitcase down so I could give Rudy some scratches on the head. "He's so cute," I said. London came up beside me and ruffled Rudy's fur. "Hi, Rudy."

The man chuckled, then said, "It's short for Rudolph. He's my good luck charm." He scratched Rudy under the chin, making Rudy's already-wagging tail pick up speed. "Rudy and I have seen some bad storms over the years and we've gotten through them all." He walked forward and put a hand on either side of Rudy's face, getting the dog's full attention. When the dog made full eye contact with him, the man said, "You back up and let our new friends inside, okay?"

When he let go of Rudy's head, the dog backed up into the cab of the truck and then jumped into the narrow back seat.

"Here," the man said, putting his hands out for our suitcases. I handed him mine and he carefully lifted it over the seat and put it in the back with Rudy. He then took London's suitcase and did the same. "Get on in."

I looked at London and she silently signaled for me to get in first. I climbed in, taking the middle seat of the front row and then London climbed in too, taking the seat next to me. It was warm—blessedly warm—in the truck. The man closed the door and walked around, taking a few moments to dust snow off the headlights.

"Benjamin…" London said, then trailed off.

"I know," I said. "I know." The man looked so much like Santa, it was uncanny. Curly white hair and a beard to match, and with him lit up from the headlights right now, I could see just how red his winter coat was. Rudy chose that moment to stick his head between our heads and sniff at my ear. I laughed and then patted his face. "It's like some sort of Christmas movie."

She laughed, but it wasn't a full laugh. She was nervous or thinking of something. To be honest, I was both nervous and thinking. Either we were in the clutches of someone who was really strange…or Santa had magically come to save us from the frigid cold and take us home.

"You don't think he's really…" I said, but trailed off. I couldn't even bring myself to say that sentence out loud. Silence descended between us as we watched the man dust snow off the second headlight, then walk around to the driver's side, open the door, and climb in.

He let out a joyful laugh as he settled into his seat. A laugh that *almost* sounded like Santa's.

"By the way," he said, turning in his seat and offering his hand, "I'm Nick."

I shook his hand. "Benjamin."

London reached around me to shake his hand and introduce herself too.

"Now," Nick said, "let's get you two home."

He brought the truck into gear and the whole thing rumbled beneath us even though we weren't moving yet. This thing was clearly very powerful. Nick put his foot on the gas pedal and we slowly moved forward. The truck took a while to build up speed, but Nick didn't want to go too fast for fear of hitting a patch of ice or, worse, not seeing a pedestrian until it was too late. The visibility was still poor.

"Thanks again for the ride," I said, as he navigated us onto the deserted bridge. I was slowly thawing in the warmth from the truck's heater, but I was still so very cold. "London and I were supposed to both fly home this morning and our partners were to join us this afternoon. But with the storm…well, our partners don't even know we're still in the state, let alone we're trying to reach them. It's been a long, cold journey and I wasn't sure I'd actually make it all the way."

"I'm sure they're miserable right now," London said. I could hear the despair in her voice. "They haven't heard from us for hours."

Nick chuckled softly and looked over at us with a twinkle in his eye. "Something tells me they're doing just fine—and they'll be thrilled to see you both. You'll still have a very merry Christmas, despite the storm."

I looked at Nick as he spoke, and when he finished and turned his attention back to the road ahead, I found I was still looking at him. I was both captivated and mystified. He looked exactly like I always pictured Santa to look when I was a kid, and he seemed to have this magical aura and warmth around him that I couldn't quite figure out.

"What about you?" London asked. "Clearing the streets on Christmas can't be what you want to be doing right now."

Nick chuckled again—he seemed to be a very joyful man. "The missus knows how important it is for me to help other people. And if that means sacrificing an evening together, she's okay with it. Why, right now, I'm sure she's laying out some milk and cookies so I have a snack when I get back home. She's very thoughtful that way. I love her so much."

"Aww…" London said.

I tried to imagine what Nick's wife looked like and the only thing I could come up with was Mrs. Claus. Nick looked at me, then smiled and winked.

Soon Nick had us over the bridge and fully into Manhattan. Here, there was a little more life—some streets had been plowed and a few cars were cautiously moving about, and there was the odd pedestrian or two hurrying through the falling snow.

"Thank you, Nick," I said as he pulled up to the curb in front of Jordan and Mandy's dorm building.

Nick shook his head. "Think nothing of it, Benjamin." He opened his door and hopped out, then hurried around to our side to open our door, helping London out and then me. Being out of the warmth of the truck and suddenly wrapped in the icy grip of the storm had me feeling like an ice cube again. My toes started aching like they were before we got in the truck. Nick stepped up on the footstep and pulled our luggage out of the back of the truck.

London gave Nick a thank you hug and then I did too. "Merry Christmas," Nick said and we repeated the greeting back to him. Then we stood and watched as he went around the truck, opened the driver's side, and climbed in. Just as we were about to turn and head into the dorm, Nick leaned over and rolled down the passenger side window. "And best wishes to Jordan and Mandy too!" he shouted. Then he rolled up the window and drove off, quickly disappearing into the snow.

I blinked several times and furiously worked my way through everything we'd said on the ride. I turned to London. "Did we ever…"

"No," she said as she shook her head quickly. "No, we didn't."

We had never mentioned Jordan's or Mandy's name. So how did…

It couldn't have been…

I shook my head. "Come on," I said. We turned around and I put my arm over London's shoulders. "Home, sweet home."

We let ourselves into the building with London's keycard and into full warmth, warmer than the truck, and took the elevator up to Jordan and Mandy's floor. Now I truly felt like I was melting, like I was turning into a human being again and I was no longer a snowman. It felt so good.

Neither one of us wanted to go back to our own dorms; we just wanted to see our partners. I could feel my heart pounding in my chest and my body felt quivery with excitement and relief.

From the elevator, we proceeded to Mandy's dorm first since it was the closest. London knocked on the door, but there was no answer. She knocked again, but with the same result. She looked at me with concern on her face.

"Maybe they're both in Jordan's dorm," I said.

We walked down the corridor and around the bend to Jordan's room, our pace a little quicker. I was worried. What if Jordan and Mandy had attempted to go to the airport and gotten stuck somewhere? What if they made it to the airport and were still there? What if all of this was for nothing?

I knocked on Jordan's door as soon as we reached it. "Jordan?" I called out. Nothing. I knocked again. "I'm worried," I said to London.

"Come on," she said. "Let's head to my dorm and get my phone—maybe we've got a message waiting." She hurried away from me toward the stairs; London was on the floor below and those stairs were much closer than the elevator.

As we turned the bend and approached the stairs, something felt off. The lights were off and the area was dark. And the furniture in the lounge had been moved from their usual spots to form a semi-circle facing the window.

"What's this?" I asked as I approached cautiously.

Chapter Eleven

Jordan

I WAS SOUNDLY ASLEEP IN THE MIDST OF some dream about Benjamin and I. It was one of those weird dreams that didn't really make sense. First, we were riding a rocket through Toronto—at least, I somehow knew it was Toronto even though I've never been—and then we were being chased by diamond thieves, because apparently, we had stolen their stolen diamond from them. Next thing I knew, Benjamin and I were in scuba suits in the coral reefs in Australia. He took off his facemask and kissed me and we kissed and kissed and kissed, and somehow we were breathing water.

It was weird. Whatever. But through it all, Benjamin was by my side. He never left.

And as I started to come out of my dream, as threads of very sleepy consciousness returned to me, I knew having Benjamin by my side was just that—a dream. He was back home and I was stuck here.

And in this semi-conscious mind space, I slowly came

to realize I was waking up because there was a hand on my shoulder, gently shaking me.

"Mandy?" I managed to mumble. I tried to pry my eyes open but they felt like they were being held closed by glue and sandpaper.

"Oh my God!" Mandy screamed. Joyful squeals followed right after.

My eyes bolted open. I stared at the face above me. I blinked. I blinked again.

"Benjamin?"

He smiled that smile that always makes my heart melt. The smile that shows off those perfect teeth and gives him a dimple in his left cheek. It's the smile I knew from being friends with him for years when we were kids and carefree. That smile had disappeared throughout much of high school. Until, that is, we started dating. Then, that smile returned.

I pushed myself up to a seated position and he had his hand on my shoulder. I'm sure I was staring at him like I didn't believe he was there. And that's because he wasn't supposed to be there. He was home with his family. The roads were closed. There was no way he could have made it back here.

Still...

"Benjamin?" I said again.

Please don't let this be a dream please don't let this be a dream please don't let this be a dream please don't let this be a—

"Hey, Jordan," he said. That sweet voice of his made my insides melt.

"Oh my God," I said. "Benjamin."

He laughed—and there was that sparkle in his eye that shows up when he's extremely happy—and then pulled me into a hug.

He's real. He's really here.

He still had his winter jacket on so there were lots of layers of fabric between us, but it still felt so right and so natural and so *good* to have him pressed against me. I hugged him tighter; I didn't want to ever let him go again.

After a very long and very tight hug, we loosened our arms enough that I could look into his handsome face. But that didn't last long before I pressed my lips to his and I kissed him, then I hugged him again.

And with my head resting on his shoulder, I finally looked past him to see Mandy…in the arms of London.

When we finally pulled apart and I made him take off his jacket and sit beside me on the couch and hold my hand under the blanket I'd spread over our knees, I asked, "How are you here?"

He let go of my hand and put his arm around my shoulders. With a few deft maneuvers, he had my head laying on his lap. I looked up at him and he stroked my hair with one hand and left the other hand to rest on my chest, right over my beating heart.

"The flight was delayed and delayed and delayed, until they finally cancelled it. From there, I spent the whole day trying to get through the storm to here…to you." His hand that was on my chest moved to stroke my chin, then he bent forward and kissed me on the mouth again. When he sat up again, he continued, "It was a crazy day. I took a taxi and we got stuck in the snow, then I walked a bit, waited forever to get into a subway car—which is where I ran into London—and then the subway kicked us all out because power was down, and we walked and walked and walked, until some kind man gave us a ride the rest of the way in his big truck."

"I thought you had gone home," I said, sounding pitiful and weak to my ears...but it made Benjamin smile that smile I loved so much.

"I wanted to text you or call you, but I lost my phone somewhere. London didn't have hers either. I wanted to call you right away, to tell you to stay here and wait for me." I could hear the love and determination in his voice, the strength that got him through that long day.

Something finally clicked. "It wouldn't have worked anyway," I said. "Cell signals are down; internet too. I couldn't even call home to find out if you'd made it there safely."

Benjamin slid down on the couch a bit, propping his feet up on the coffee table. Across from us, Mandy and London were similarly snuggling and whispering to each other, their words interrupted by occasional kisses. With Benjamin sliding down the couch a bit, into a semi-sitting-semi-lying-down position, I moved up to lay my head on his stomach to keep staring into his beautiful eyes.

"I'm glad I didn't make it," he said. He started stroking my hair again. "It wouldn't be Christmas without you."

I reached up and stroked his face, running my fingertips across his stubbly jaw. "I'm so happy you're here.

I still find it hard to believe, like it's all too good to be true."

"It's true, baby. I'm really here," he said.

"Having you here is the best Christmas present ever," I told him. He beamed that smile back at me.

On the other side of the lounge area, a burst of girlish giggles erupted. Benjamin looked over at them.

"Sorry," London said, giggling again. I rolled my head to the side to look over at them; London was sitting in Mandy's lap, the blanket pulled up over both of them. "Mandy was telling me about the cookies you baked and, well, I think she told you about the brownies she once tried."

I chuckled. "She did." I looked up at Benjamin and his clueless expression. "Somehow when she baked brownies, they exploded."

His eyes went wide with disbelief, but he smiled. "What I heard in all of that, though, is you made cookies?"

I laughed. "You haven't eaten much today, have you?"

He shook his head. "We split a bagel hours ago, but that was it."

I reached over to the coffee table and my finger snagged the edge of the plate. I pulled it closer, then picked up the biggest cookie I could find. I broke off a piece and slipped it into Benjamin's mouth. He chewed and swallowed, grinning the whole time. Then I fed him the next piece.

"It's very good," he said after swallowing down that bite. I gave him another piece.

"We had time to kill. And somehow the Rainbow

Club kitchen had all the ingredients." I shook my head lightly, still not quite figuring how all that worked out.

"And the tree?" Benjamin asked, nodding his head toward the coffee table.

I slipped the last piece of the cookie into his mouth and then said, "I don't know. It was also in the Rainbow Club. Everyone else with keys is long gone, so Mandy can't figure it out. It's almost like magic, like maybe Santa did it or something."

There was an odd look on Benjamin's face and he just kind of stared at me for a moment.

"What?" I said. After a beat, I felt the need to say, "I don't actually believe in Santa…you know that, right?"

He shook his head, his eyes closing briefly. "Sorry. It's just today has been full of really weird coincidences that I kept thinking bordered on some sort of Christmas magic. A woman pulled me on the train to meet London and then disappeared. I later met the cab driver's husband. But the…" He paused and sort of narrowed his eyes at me, like he was deciding if he should tell me something. "But the biggest sort of magic Santa thing was the guy that picked us up in his truck. Nick, as in Saint Nicholas, and his dog Rudy, as in short for Rudolph, in a truck that said North Pole on it. He looked *exactly* like Santa. And then after he dropped us off, he said to wish merry Christmas to you and Mandy…but we had never told him your names, yet he somehow knew them."

Any other night, I would have brushed that all off as weird coincidences and just the mind trying to make connections that didn't exist. But tonight…after the

Christmas tree and the cookie ingredients and the odd way in which this disaster of a holiday turned into perhaps the most perfect one yet…I was willing to believe for one night maybe magic and Santa both exist.

I told this to Benjamin. Then I said, "But whatever brought us together for Christmas—whether it was magic, pure coincidence, or the guiding hand of Santa—all that matters is I have you and you have me."

"I have a gift for you," he whispered.

I grinned. "I have one for you too, but right now you're the only gift I want and need."

"I love you," he said.

"I love you too."

He kissed me and I kissed him.

About Dylan James

Dylan James believes love is for everyone, and through writing gay young adult romances, he hopes to get that point across to younger readers. Dylan is a lover of books, Star Trek, and animals. He lives in Canada with his husband and two cats.

Dylan also writes adult gay romances under the name Cameron D. James.

Follow Dylan on Twitter (DylanJamesYA) and Instagram (DylanJamesYA).

More by Dylan James

Gay Love and Other Fairy Tales
Gay Love and Other Christmas Magic
Thunder

More From Deep Hearts YA

Gay Love and Other Fairy Tales
Dylan James

What starts with a surprise kiss leads to a year of shared secrets, hidden love, relationship troubles, and broken hearts. For football captain Benjamin Cooper and his secret boyfriend, cheer co-captain Jordan Ortiz, there's only one thing standing in the way of their love—Ben's intense need to stay closeted, a need that just might tear them apart.

Available in ebook and paperback!

Thunder
Dylan James

Grant Peters is sixteen and making a name for himself on the local rodeo circuit. His only concern is Logan Summers, the only boy who can match—and beat!—his times in calf roping. But when his world gets shaken up and there's a very real chance that Grant and his family will have to sell the farm and move to the city, leaving behind everything he's ever known, Grant sets off on a dangerous journey to save everything.

Available in ebook and paperback!

The Killing Spell

Shane Ulrrein

Edward Peach is a fourteen-year-old wizard who receives a letter that he has been accepted into the prestigious Prymoutekhny Wizards Academy for Boys, in the faraway land of Aradia. His parents are overjoyed, but he feels reluctant to leave his family, friends, and his comfy cottage in the English coastal village of Manley.

As term begins, Edward adjusts to life in his new school, dealing with bullies, strict teachers, and challenging wizardry classes. He is almost ready to give up when he falls in love with a charismatic, privileged boy—and talented wizard—named Mr. Andreas. Prymoutekhny is a school that has still not opened up to same-sex attraction, so he must keep his feelings secret.

Soon, Edward and the impressive boy realize their deep attraction for each other. This causes immediate controversy in the school, as they are the first two boys from feuding houses to come together—especially in a school where house rivalry can end in murder.

Available in ebook and paperback!

Made in the USA
Middletown, DE
30 December 2019

82213315R00070